Good-by to Stony Crick

illustrated by Deanne Hollinger

# Good-by to Stony Crick

## by Kathryn Borland
## & Helen Speicher

McGRAW-HILL BOOK COMPANY
New York   St. Louis   San Francisco
Düsseldorf   Johannesburg   Kuala Lumpur   London
Mexico   Montreal   New Delhi   Panama   Rio de Janeiro
Singapore   Sydney   Toronto

**Library of Congress Cataloging in Publication Data**

Borland, Kathryn Kilby.
  Good-by to Stony Crick.

  SUMMARY: When the family is forced by fire and
poverty to leave their Appalachian home, Jeremy finds
city life in Chicago and its effect on his family hard
to bear.
  [1. City and town life—Fiction.    2. Family life
—Fiction]    I. Speicher, Helen Ross, joint author.
II.    Hollinger, Deanne, illus.    III.  Title.
PZ7.B64847Go      [Fic]      74-11457

ISBN 0-07-006532-2

123456789   MUBP   7898765

# Contents

# 1

# Good-by to Stony Crick

Jeremy sat cross-legged at the back of the old blue station wagon, swaying back and forth as the car bumped along the narrow, rutted road. The honey-sweet fragrance of clover drifted in through the open windows, and he drew a deep breath while he stared back at the knobby hills and groves of pine and spruce, knowing he might never see them again. He was glad the road here along the crick was twisty so Pa couldn't drive the car any faster, not that it could have gone much faster anyhow, chock-full as it was of kids and boxes and baskets.

He had never thought the time would come when he'd be sorry if he knew he'd never see the schoolhouse again, but when they got to it, he felt sad. The crooked old, black shutters were closed over the windows of the little weather-stained building for the summer, and the grass around it was knee-deep.

He thought he heard a whistle, and sure enough there was Pete Eustis cutting through the grass on his way to the crick. He waved his fishpole at them and grinned, even if Johnson had blacked his eye the last time he saw Pete.

Jeremy balanced himself to wave back to Pete and get one more look at the schoolhouse. Johnson had his head stuck out of a side window, his carroty-red hair blown straight back from a round face that was as freckled as a turkey egg. Nobody'd better ever make fun of Johnson's freckles though.

"Johnson Weatherhead, you pull your head back in there this minute," Ma ordered from her seat next to Pa in the front of the station wagon. The five Weatherhead children were crowded together in the back.

"How would you feel if another car come along and cut it spang off?" Ma always asked this at the beginning of a ride, so that much hadn't changed anyway.

"Yeah, stupid!" Ethan jeered. "A dumb head's better than none." With all those boxes and baskets in between him and Johnson he felt safe.

You'd never guess Ethan and Johnson were twins. Ethan was as dark as Jeremy and pretty near as tall, even if Jeremy was eleven and the twins were nine. Johnson was half a head shorter.

"I don't want you boys giving any trouble," Pa spoke up suddenly, surprising them. "We got a long, hot day's drive ahead of us before we get to Chicago." Pa gunned the motor, stirring up a breeze that was heavy with the smell of damp earth.

Jeremy knew Ma had cried last night, because he'd heard her, but he didn't know how Pa felt about moving to Chicago. He looked at Pa's broad shoulders next to Ma's thin ones. Pa's hair was black and curly like Jeremy's, and anybody around always felt better when Pa's big laugh rang out. He was never scared or tired or cross. Not even the night of the fire.

*2*

"We'll be back, won't we, Pa?" Jeremy had to ask.

"Sure," Pa said in his easy voice. "Sure we will. You know we'll be back just as soon as we get enough money laid by. But what makes you so sure you won't like Chicago?"

Did that mean Pa thought he'd like it there?

"I bet we never come back. We'll always stay in Chicago," Ethan said. He didn't sound like he minded.

Caroline's face puckered up. She was six, and never needed much of any reason to cry. She started to bawl now, and Ma reached back to pat one of her yellow braids. "No use grievin' over what's left behind. Reckon that's why Lot's wife was put in the Bible," she told her.

"Who's Lot's wife?" Johnson asked.

"Johnson Weatherhead," Ma said, "don't you ever listen on Sunday morning?"

"You know he don't, Ma," said Caroline. "He don't listen at church and I'll bet he don't listen at school. He don't do nothing but fight."

Johnson doubled up his fists. "How'd you like something different to cry about?"

Ma swatted at him, but he ducked. Ma had almost as many freckles as Johnson, but her face was thin instead of round, and her straight hair, pulled into a bun at the back of her neck, was brown. Jeremy hadn't noticed till lately that there were little threads of gray in it.

"We're not out of Stony Crick," she said, "and you're fightin' already. You five young'uns have got to get along or we'll be clean out of our minds before ever we get to Chicago."

"Chicago," Homer D. laughed. "Chicago." He'd burrowed under the pile of blankets, and with his head stuck out from under them, he looked like a comical little turtle.

Jeremy always had to smile at Homer D. Once Johnson had knocked Joe Eustis down when he'd said Homer D. looked like a monkey, but Jeremy had to admit he really did a little. Maybe it was the way he kind of crouched along when he walked, or the way his jaw stuck out from his face. But even if Homer D. wasn't very bright or very good-looking, anybody that saw his grin had to grin back.

"I'm hungry," Ethan complained. "When we going to eat?"

"It won't be just half a mile from home and this early in the morning, I can promise you that," Ma told him. "The food we got's got to last a while."

"We're starvin', Ma. Look we cain't even sit up." But Ethan couldn't prove it because there wasn't room for him to lie down.

Jeremy shrugged impatiently. He didn't feel the least bit hungry. No one of the Weatherheads had ever been in a big city, much less lived in one. Not even Pa. Now Jeremy didn't see how Ethan and Johnson could leave Blue Mountain without thinking about anything but filling their stomachs.

They were already at the crossroads where Posey Martin's store was, and out of the corner of his eye he could see Ma looking back at the one-story, gray building the same way he was. Ma'd always wanted to have a store because she'd grown up helping in her Uncle Foster's at Abbott's Crossing. Pa said he'd just as soon they had a store if Ma could find somebody that wanted to sell one and figure out how to buy it. He'd really been caught between a rock and a hard place when Posey Martin said he'd sell and Ma started her savings jar. Last fall when Pa'd had the good job working on the new highway, Ma's saving jar was almost full to the top with dimes and

*4*

quarters and even quite a few dollar bills. But Pa'd lost that job, and even before the fire, the jar was almost empty. With small change, it would take a long time to fill a Mason jar.

It was a shame for Posey Martin to have that store when he didn't seem to care two pins about it. Half a dozen cane-seated chairs stood on the front porch, but the bottoms were out of most of them, and the cement steps down to the road were broken and crumbling. Ma'd planned to change all that.

Jeremy remembered how bare and scorched their own doorstep was by the fire. That doorstep was every bit there was left of their house.

The fire had probably started from a spark from the open fireplace. What would have happened if it hadn't been for Henry, nobody knew. Ma'd said a house was no place for a raccoon, but she'd finally let Jeremy keep Henry inside till his lame leg healed. The night of the fire Henry had scrabbled and snuffled around in his box till he woke up Jeremy, and that's how he came to smell the smoke. He'd leaped out of bed and opened the door to the front room. Big tongues of yellow-and-red fire were licking at the walls and the floor out there, and he'd slammed the door shut and pounded on the wall to wake Pa and Ma and Caroline in the next room. Pa'd hollered for the boys to get themselves out the window, and they'd all slid down the hill and stood there just watching their house go. Pa'd managed to drag out the chest Ma kept her quilts and heirloom things in, but they didn't save another thing except that and their skins.

"I hope we're doing right moving to Chicago." Ma's voice brought him back to the present. "Maybe it's not as easy to get a job as Fenn says. You know Fenn."

Jeremy wondered about tall, quick-tongued Fenn. Pa'd said once that his cousin Fenn could talk his way out of a deadfall trap, and he probably could. Ever since he'd moved to Chicago, though, Fenn had been pestering Pa to move up there, without any luck till now.

Pa laughed, but it was a short, choked sound, not like his usual laugh. "Fenn's all right. You just have to know how much to believe. I'm not green enough to think he can get me a hundred dollars a week like he says, but he'll come up with something. Besides, what else is there for us to do? There's no way in the world for us to get by at Stony Crick with no house and no job and nothing laid by."

"The neighbors said they'd help raise us a house," Ma said in a small voice.

"You got to have something to raise before anybody can help raise it, and we can't go on fallin' further and further behind." Pa's jaw was set in the way that meant he didn't intend to talk about it any more.

At a fork in the road Pa turned the station wagon away from the crick, and Jeremy could see Uncle Frank Dawson weeding outside his sagging wire fence. He straightened up to wave at them, and Jeremy wondered who was going to wave to them in Chicago.

On Clay Lick Road something furry scurried into the underbrush, and that made him wish he could feel Henry's coarse fur under his fingers. The Eustis boys swore up and down they'd take good care of Henry, but you couldn't set much store by a Eustis promise.

Soon they were far enough along on their way so he didn't know where every path went. The roads went down into hollows and climbed back out again all morning, but the trees were still festooned with wild grapevine that would make good swinging and there were long stretches between the small, weathered houses, like at home. Then all of a sudden there was a noise like a woodchuck caught in a trap, and the station wagon lurched over to the side of the road and stopped.

# 2

## In Between

"Hit's that no-good fan belt again," Pa said. "Might've knowed it'd never get us to Chicago without bustin'."

"I'm hungry," Johnson whined.

"Me too," Ethan echoed.

"Whatever we got we can only eat it once," Pa said. "So go ahead and eat it whilst I fix the fan belt."

"Will Weatherhead," Ma snapped, "you know as well as I do if we let these young'uns eat every time they say they're hungry, every crumb we got'll be gone by night-fall."

"Shucks, Ma," Johnson begged, "just let us eat now and we won't be hungry again till you say it's time."

"Well, all right." Ma didn't look convinced, but they all boiled out of the car like corn when you took the lid off the popper. Jeremy still wasn't too hungry, but it felt good to get out of that cramped car where every time you tried to move, you stuck your foot in a bucket or got stabbed in the back with a broom handle.

"Get one of the big baskets and the kettle of boiled potatoes out of the car," Ma told Jeremy.

"What's in the basket, Ma? What's in it?" Caroline was jumping up and down, her yellow braids bobbing back and forth.

"I reckon that's the one Miz Addison give us, with the green apple pies in it."

"Hit was right good of the neighbors to give us sich a send-off," Pa said, his dark head still bent over the engine. "Looks like there's enough there to last us all winter."

"Not if we eat every two hours, it won't," Ma said.

Caroline helped Ma spread a faded, pink cotton blanket under a big oak tree with wide, outstretched branches.

They couldn't wait to see what was in that basket.

"Ugh! Dry grits." Johnson made a face.

"Grits." Homer D. grinned. He grabbed a handful and crammed them into his mouth before Ma could stop him. The face he made was so funny everybody had to laugh, even Homer D. once he'd spit out the grits.

Aside from the apple pie and a loaf of bread, Jeremy couldn't see too much in that basket you could sink your teeth into right off. Mostly there were things like the grits and cornmeal and a sack of salt and some dried beans.

"Heck," Ethan said, "we'd ought to opened Miz Fenner's basket instead. There's not much in this one."

"Ethan Weatherhead," Ma said, "don't let me hear any more of such ungrateful talk. It was nice enough of Miz Addison to keep all seven of us at her house for two whole weeks, let alone send along such a nice basket to take with us."

"Us," Homer D. echoed, putting his hands on his hips just the way Ma did. "Us."

"It's going to be a real feast," Ma said, "with the boiled

potatoes I brought, and Miz Addison's good bread and pie. Wasn't it a mercy our potato crop was so good this year? We won't want for potatoes for a long time to come."

Ethan and Caroline ate their potatoes out of their hands, but Jeremy and Johnson made potato sandwiches out of theirs. They managed to get two apiece before Ma clapped the lid back on the kettle. Ethan gulped his pie down and then snatched the crust Johnson was saving till last and made off with it down the road. Johnson took out after Ethan, and Jeremy ran along behind just to see what would happen.

All of a sudden there was an almighty rustling and thrashing around in the brush alongside the road and a big shaggy dog shot out and ran straight at Jeremy, barking and jumping. Jeremy froze, petrified, while Johnson and Ethan ran off down the road without paying any attention.

"Down, Arlo!"

Jeremy was afraid to take his eyes off the dog to see where the voice had come from. But the dog had already lost interest in him and had raced back to a tall, gaunt man stepping out of the brush behind him.

The man, who was cradling a gun under one arm, watched Jeremy with lively black eyes. "Arlo wouldn't bite you even if you bit him first, son."

Jeremy tried to smile, but the dog was looking back in his direction, and he couldn't bear the thought of the big animal jumping toward him again. Jeremy was standing beside the station wagon, so he hopped in and slammed the door behind him. Ethan and Johnson had run back to where the blanket was under the tree, but they'd never noticed that he was gone, what with their wrangling and the dog barking and Homer D. banging the lid up and down on the potato kettle.

So far, nobody'd noticed how scared Jeremy was every time he saw a dog. They probably wouldn't even remember when Uncle Frank's dog, Old Bones, bit him, but he'd never forget it as long as he lived. Ethan and Johnson would really have him over a barrel if they knew they could scare him with the least dog that ever was.

After the hullabaloo quieted down, Pa and the man talked for a while, until he said he had to go on. Then Pa fixed the fan belt and finished his dinner, and they all piled back in the car.

One by one all the young'uns except Jeremy dozed off, even if there wasn't room to stretch out. It was the longest afternoon Jeremy'd ever put in. They were off the winding roads and onto a big concrete highway now. There were more cars here, driving faster, and it grieved him to see so many little dead creatures along the side of the road. Hardly a mile went by that he didn't see a woodchuck or a raccoon or a possum that would never run or climb a tree again.

The heat rolled off the sun-baked concrete in little waves. Ma's green dress was wet between her shoulder blades. In fact, every last one of them felt like they'd just got out of the river and put their clothes on before they were dry.

Sometime around midafternoon, Jeremy heard Johnson moving behind him. "Wouldn't that old crick be nice to jump into now?" he said.

"Wonder how many fish Pete caught?" Ethan tried to stick his head out of the window, but before he got it halfway out, Ma snapped at him to get it back in the car. She must have eyes in the back of her head. She didn't even turn around.

"I'm thirsty," Caroline whined.

Ethan joined in. "Me, too. When we going to have supper?"

This time Ma did turn around, shoving her damp hair away from her forehead. "Remember what you promised."

"Johnson promised," Ethan put in. "How'd he know whether the rest of us would get hungry or not?"

"We'll stop when it's supper time, and not before," Ma told them firmly.

"We won't stop atall," Pa said. "We're on the big highway now, and there's no place to stop. We'll have to eat as we go or not at all."

"What if we have to go to the bathroom?" Johnson asked.

"I have to," Caroline said. "Right now!"

"You should have thought of that sooner," Pa told her, but in a few minutes there was a sign that said "Rest Area," and he pulled the car off the road.

"Couldn't we stay and run around here for a while?" Ethan begged. "I can't hardly straighten up."

"We can't stop here a second longer than we have to," Pa answered. "We'll be doing good if we get to Chicago by nightfall as it is."

When they all got back in the car, it seemed like forever to Jeremy before Ma decided it was time for supper. Then she just opened the kettle and passed around cold potatoes.

"Just cold potatoes and that's all?" Ethan asked.

"If you're as hungry as you claim, they'll taste good enough," Pa told him.

They were still eating when they began going past dingy factories and tall smokestacks. Their road joined with another wide road, and the cars thundered along four

*12*

abreast in both directions. Jeremy bet even Pa was in a cold sweat; if anything happened to their car here, the ones behind would roll right over them and nobody'd ever know the Weatherheads had tried to make it to Chicago. Some places there were roads underneath, and some places there were roads overhead, and every inch was covered with cars. Something was bound to happen with so many going so fast in so many different directions. Jeremy knew now just how a possum felt when the hounds were after it.

"Is this Chicago?" Caroline asked.

"This is Chicago." If Jeremy didn't know Pa was never scared of anything, he'd think his voice sounded scared now.

# 3

## Chicago

"Whew!" Ethan held his nose. "If this is Chicago, it sure smells rotten. Run the window up."

"It's up as far as it'll go," Johnson said. "I'm kind of gettin' used to the smell now. It's not so bad."

Jeremy didn't see how anybody could get used to breathing such air, let alone a person raised in Stony Crick. And just as bad as the smell was the noise. There were so many different ones, he couldn't separate them out. Hundreds of cars and trucks and buses rumbled and roared all round them, and once in a while a train even thundered along right over their heads. Occasionally there was an angry blast from a horn as a car swept around them, and every once in a while there was a high, wailing sound that Pa said was from an ambulance or a police car. Somehow their station wagon and all the people in it seemed shrunken. They were carried along on the wave of noise like a little cork spinning helplessly down a river.

After a while Ma said, "It's gettin' on for dark. Will, you got that paper Fenn sent us with the directions on it?"

"It hasn't hardly had time to get lost since the last time you asked me." Pa laughed, but it still wasn't his old good-feeling laugh.

By now he'd managed to get the car off the big highway and onto the narrower city streets. Tall, dark, brick buildings rose high along both sides of them, and people scurried back and forth on the hot sidewalks like ants boiling up out of an anthill.

They drove down street after street, Pa and Ma craning their necks to read the little signs up on the high poles.

"It's unpossible," Pa finally said. "Ever time I slow down to read one of the pesky things, somebody barrels up behind and honks like we had the whole of Chicago bottled up. And there's no place to stop, so what am I supposed to do?"

Just then a big truck lumbered away from the curb ahead of them, and Pa eased the station wagon into the space.

"Here, Jeremy," he said, "show this paper to somebody and ask how we find this street. The rest of you stay put."

Jeremy climbed out of the car with the paper in his hand. He waited for somebody to slow down enough so he could show it. Finally a short, fat man stopped to pull a handkerchief out of his pocket and wipe off his forehead. He really looked hot. His shirt collar was unbuttoned, his tie was loosened, and his gray jacket hung limply over his arm.

Jeremy walked up to him and held out the paper.

"Could you please—" he began, but the man pushed his hand aside and hurried on down the walk without so much as a word.

"Well I'll be a monkey's uncle," Pa said.

Ma said, "I hope everybody in Chicago's not that unmannerly."

A white-haired man who'd been watching from the doorway of a little lunchroom came across the walk now.

"Thought maybe I could help you." He reached out his hand for Jeremy's paper.

He frowned at it and finally said, "I don't have the slightest idea where it is, but I see Joe across the street. He'll know."

Joe turned out to be a policeman, and of all things, he was black. Ethan and Johnson had their heads and shoulders stuck out of the window and their mouths wide open. This was a real policeman just like the ones in their reading books. They'd always thought of a policeman as something they'd never see any more than they would an elf or a giant. And if they ever did see one, they wouldn't have expected him to be black.

Ma'd always told them not to stare, and maybe she wasn't staring now, but she was looking at Joe pretty hard out of the corner of her eye while he set them straight.

The boys were bubbling over when Jeremy got back in the car.

"Pete Eustis told me Chicago was full of black people," Ethan said. "And he said we better watch out for them. Wonder how one of them got to be a policeman?"

Pa turned around in the seat and frowned at them. "Just like anybody else got to be one. And there's no better time than now to tell you that Pete was partly right, but only partly. We're gonna meet up with a lot of black people here, but as for watchin' out for 'em, they're good and bad same as anybody else, and don't you forget it."

Joe had managed to set them straight, but they still had quite a way to go, down street after street of tall buildings and store fronts, their street windows covered with heavy iron bars.

*16*

"They got a jail in every block," Ethan said.

"No," Pa laughed. "Them's stores. Fenn told how a store is liable to get cleaned out in one night unless there's bars to the windows."

"Well I never," Ma said. "Such a place."

They were beginning to think they'd be driving all night when Ma said, "That's it. That's the street."

A lamp on a tall pole gave out just enough light so they could see the numbers on the big buildings.

"I hope we live up at the very top," Caroline said.

But when they found the number Fenn had sent them, it turned out to be a gray, frame house squeezed in between two of the tall buildings. A skimpy porch with a spindly little railing stretched across the front, and three, wide, wooden steps climbed up to it. It didn't have a friendly look, maybe because the only light came from a window at one side of the front door. All the other windows, upstairs and down, were dark. There were cans and paper trash all over the sidewalk, and in the narrow space between this house and the building next door was an old rusted-out bedspring.

Caroline hollered, "I'm goin' to be the first one in!"

Homer D. followed her out of the car, giggling.

"In," he said, "in."

Caroline caught her toe in a loose board on one of the steps and started to bawl, which she was very good at. A tall, black-haired lady came running out of the house and tried to pick her up. At that Jeremy was sure they could hear Caroline back at Stony Crick.

"Hush," the lady kept saying crossly, "hush," but Caroline wouldn't.

"I'm much obliged to you," Ma told the lady, "but Caroline just never will take to a stranger."

"You must be the Weatherheads that rented the up-stairs." The lady didn't sound any too happy about it. She was staring at the young'uns piling out of the station wagon. "How many of you are there anyway?"

"There's seven of us," Ma answered. "Did you say upstairs? Fenn didn't tell us nothin' about the house. We didn't know we'd live upstairs or that we wouldn't have a whole house to ourselves."

"House to yourselves?" The lady smiled just with her mouth. "You're lucky to have what you've got. I never rented to anybody but teachers before last year, but now the neighborhood's so run-down most of them won't live here any more. The only one left's Mr. Sherman. I never in the world rented to hill—Not to anybody from Kentucky before this year, and the Buckhorns and their kin, that moved in here, proved I was right. But once you let down the bars, it's too late. Did I tell you I'm Mrs. Quill?"

Ma ran her hand across her forehead. "You mean there's more than us going to live up there? How many?"

"There's about eight of the Buckhorns as near as I can tell. They're down home visiting now, but they'll be back soon enough. Their kin went back to stay; they're the ones that lived in your part."

"Are any of those Buckhorns girls?" Caroline asked.

"Every one of them," Mrs. Quill said, "all six. And if you're smart, you won't have anything to do with any of them."

"You got any girls?" Caroline had forgotten that Mrs. Quill was a stranger.

"One."

"What's her name? I could play with her till the others get back."

"Her name's Jean Elizabeth, and she stays pretty close to home."

Two boys about Ethan's and Johnson's size raced by on the sidewalk. When they got a little way past the house one of them stuck out his tongue and the other one hollered, "Mrs. Quill, call the cops; you got a tongue that never stops!"

Mrs. Quill's face turned red and her eyes narrowed. "Hillbillies," she muttered with a sniff.

Ma stiffened. "Reckon we'll look at our rooms now." She started up the steps, but Mrs. Quill shook her head.

"No need for you to come through the front part," she said. "You got your own stairway around in the back."

They squeezed past the rusty bedsprings, and Mrs. Quill showed them a rickety stairway that led up into the dark. She just left them there without so much as a good night.

The boys raced up and down the stairs two or three times while Ma and Pa went up once. Homer D. wouldn't climb up at all. He wouldn't let Pa carry him up, either. He just sat there on the bottom step, and Pa said he'd come back and get him later. Homer D. never would take to anything new, and he'd never been in a house with an upstairs before.

When they got the door open, Jeremy thought maybe Homer D. was right. Their part of the house wasn't much to look at. Pa pulled on the light string, and at least a dozen big brown bugs scuttled across the floor and disappeared. The floor looked to be covered with brown linoleum, but it was so dirty nobody could tell for sure. There were three rooms. The kitchen was the biggest. It had a stove and a sink with faucets, like Ma wanted. A big icebox stood in one corner, but the door hung crooked and it didn't look to be good for much. In the other end of the kitchen were two dirty chairs upholstered in dark red, with seats that sagged almost to the floor. Near the stove was a shabby table with yellow paint peeling off to show blue paint underneath. Six rickety chairs to match were drawn up to it.

The other two rooms were for sleeping. A big brass bed almost filled up one of them, and there was a brown-painted bed, a little smaller, in the other one.

"Fenn said this place had furniture in it, but it sure don't amount to much," Pa said.

Ma just looked around without saying a word for a spell. Then she said, "You boys go down and git my bucket and mop outen the car."

Pa looked at her like she'd taken leave of her senses. "You're not fixin' to scrub tonight, late as it is?" he asked her. "Let's get our blankets in and have us a good night's sleep first."

Ma looked at him like he was one of those bugs. "Maybe you can sleep in such a place, but I wouldn't even set down, let alone stretch out to sleep."

Jeremy thought it didn't look a whole lot different after it was mopped, but Ma set a whole lot of store by mopping.

There were two extra doors in the place, and Caroline peeked through both of them as fast as she could. One of them opened into a big cubbyhole that Ma said was to keep clothes in. The other one opened into a long, dark hall.

"Shut that door, Caroline," Ma said. "That part don't belong to us."

Caroline's face had the crumpled look it always had before she was about to cry.

"What's the matter?" Jeremy asked her.

"I thought we'd have a real bathroom with a big white tub," Caroline sobbed, "but there isn't any at all."

20

Ma stood still for a minute. "Why, so there isn't. Did you see one out back?" she asked Pa.

"Can't say's I did," Pa said, "but I got to go down to get Homer D. and I'll scout around. You boys can come down and fetch the bedclothes out of the car. Jeremy, you stay and help your Ma."

Pa and the boys came back in a few minutes. Homer D. was fast asleep, and Pa was carrying him over his shoulder. He shook his head.

"Not a sign of one," he said. "Don't that beat all?"

"Sometimes Fenn don't have sense enough to pour sand out of a boot," Ma said crossly.

"Now, Harriet," Pa said, "no need to mean-mouth Fenn. He done the best he could. You can ask Miz Quill about it in the morning."

Ma sniffed and started unrolling the bedclothes. "I won't ask Miz Quill anything if I can help it," she said.

Ma and Pa and Caroline slept in the room with the big brass bed, and the boys took the other one. Ethan and Johnson got in a fight about who would sleep in the bed. They made so much noise with their squabbling that Ma came in and said the four boys would take turns two-by-two, and anybody she heard a peep out of wouldn't get to sleep in the bed for a week, maybe never.

# 4

## Baron

Ma did ask Mrs. Quill about the bathroom after all. When Jeremy woke up in the morning, the bedroom door was open a little bit and he could see the two of them in the kitchen. Mrs. Quill was giving Ma's mop and bucket, leaning up against the wall, the once-over. Then she opened the door to the hall and pointed to another door at the end of it.

"That's your bathroom down at the end of the hall," she said. "You'll share it with the Buckhorns." Butter wouldn't melt in her mouth this morning.

"Didn't you say there was eight of them?" Ma asked.

"You'll just have to get up early in the morning," Mrs. Quill laughed. "They won't bother you much taking up time in the bathtub anyhow."

Then she showed Ma how to light the stove. Ma told her the icebox wouldn't work.

"I can't hardly afford to fix it with what you pay me," Mrs. Quill told her. "If you want to have it fixed, you can."

The rooms weren't much lighter now than they had

been last night. After Mrs. Quill left, Jeremy got up. There wasn't any window in the boys' room, but he could hardly wait to find out what he could see from the windows in the other rooms.

If this was Chicago, it surely wasn't much to set eyes on. The kitchen window was at the back of the house. Down below was the yard, where Pa had moved their car after Mrs. Quill told him he couldn't park in front of the building. There were two other cars there, both of them without tires. Jeremy couldn't see a blade of grass anywhere—just hard-packed dirt and cement.

Across a narrow street were more buildings like the ones on either side of their house. A thin, black cat pawed through the garbage from an overturned metal can, and two little boys were chasing each other up and down the street. The window in Pa's and Ma's room opened right out onto a brick wall. If Jeremy was to put his hand out of the window, he could touch that other wall.

Ma'd cooked up a big mess of grits, and everybody but Jeremy was full of talk.

"What's the matter, Jeremy? Cat got your tongue?" Pa asked finally.

"Guess so," Jeremy said. He wished this was a dream, but it wasn't. This ugly apartment in this smelly city was where they were to live, and he wasn't ever going to wake up and be anywhere else.

He was glad when there was a knock at the door and Fenn came in, smiling and sure of himself as always.

"See you made it all right," Fenn said. "I'd almost give up on you."

"We pretty near didn't make it, but we're here," Pa told him. "I hope you're not fixin' to say I got to work today, because I don't know when I've been so tuckered out."

Fenn cleared his throat. "Well," he said, "my land, I

wouldn't have knowed any of you young'uns. Every one of you's growed a foot since I saw you last."

"About that job—" Pa said.

Fenn looked around the kitchen. "Reckon the place could do with a mite of fixin' up," he said, "but it was the best I could do."

Pa tried to catch Fenn's eye. "You did get a job for me?" he asked.

"Job," Homer D. repeated, as he eyed Fenn cautiously from behind one of the big red chairs.

"Well." Fenn didn't look at Pa. "I run into a little trouble. Seems they're layin' off instead of hirin' right now."

"Where does that leave me?" Pa asked. Jeremy'd never heard Pa sound so worried before.

"There's plenty of jobs in Chicago," Fenn said, "just not at our plant, that's all. You won't have no trouble. If you can't get a job in Chicago, you can't get one anywheres. I come by early this morning to take you by the employment office."

Pa went to the bathroom to slick down his hair and put on his clean shirt, and then he went off with Fenn. Ma started clearing off the table, but she wasn't singing like she did at home. She kept them all busy one way and another. Jeremy and Ethan and Johnson carried kettles and baskets and sacks upstairs, and Caroline washed the dishes.

Ma started in on the windows right away.

"Why bother?" Jeremy asked her. "You won't see nothing but that brick wall."

"Then we're going to see it through a clean window," Ma said.

Jeremy'd ought to know he was wasting his breath

*24*

trying to keep Ma from washing windows. Nothing perked Ma up like clean windows. Before she got through she was even singing "Beulah Land."

Caroline tugged on Ma's skirt. "She's down there," she said.

"Who?" Ma gave the window an extra polish and frowned. "A lot of that dirt's on the outside," she said.

"Miz Quill's girl, Jean Elizabeth. Miz Quill said she kept her close to home, but she's down there now."

Before Ma could say anything Caroline raced downstairs, and that was the last they saw of her all morning.

Toward noon Ma said, "Jeremy, you go down and hunt up Caroline. She'll have her welcome wore out before we've been here a day. Besides, it's most near dinner time, and I don't want that Miz Quill thinkin' she has to feed my young'un."

Jeremy took his time. He could see Ma was going to work the spots off them all day.

There was no sign of Caroline any place in the back yard or around in the front, either. He climbed up the front steps and onto the porch. The door was open, and he could see into a dark hall with a door on either side. He walked in and was trying to decide which door to knock on when he heard a noise like a growl, and something big and black came padding toward him from the far end of the hall. It was the biggest, blackest dog he'd ever laid eyes on. It just kept coming, coming, slow and easy, straight toward him. Jeremy backed up against the wall. He could feel sweat rolling down between his shoulder blades, and he couldn't pull his feet up from the floor.

This dog didn't look a bit like Old Bones, but all of a sudden he felt as if it was Old Bones coming toward him. The day it had happened he'd been at Uncle Frank's.

When he went into the house for a drink of water, he hadn't seen Old Bones stretched out just inside the door, and he'd stepped on him. Bones hadn't made a sound— just reared up like a snake and buried his teeth deep in Jeremy's ankle. He'd had to grit his teeth to keep from bawling when Uncle Frank washed the blood off with yellow soap, but worse than that was the way the dog had looked just before he bit him. Bones had always been so gentle that Jeremy would as soon have expected Uncle Frank to sink his teeth into his ankle. And here Bones was, baring his long yellow fangs and acting like he'd as soon tear Jeremy apart as look at him.

If Old Bones would do that, what could he expect from a dog that had never seen him before? And this big black dog kept coming straight at him.

Just when he thought he'd have to holler if he could, the door across from where he stood opened and a tall, thin man with blond hair appeared in the doorway. The dog padded up to him, still making a sort of half-growl in his throat. The man leaned over and patted him.

"What's the matter, Baron?" he asked. "Do we have company?"

The man acted as though he didn't even see Jeremy there. That made him feel creepy, and he started to tiptoe away. Then the thin man raised his head, and Jeremy could see that he was blind.

"Who's there?" he asked in a friendly way.

"Jeremy Weatherhead. I live upstairs."

"I'm John Sherman. I heard you moving in last night."

"I'm trying to find my sister. I thought she might be at Miz Quill's."

"Mrs. Quill and Jean Elizabeth went out a while ago,

probably to the grocery. Maybe they took your sister along. Why don't you wait for them in here?"

Mr. Sherman stepped aside, but the big dog blocked the doorway. He sat quietly staring at them, his long red tongue lolling out of his mouth.

Jeremy didn't know what to do. He wasn't about to walk past that dog. Then Mr. Sherman made it easier for him. He snapped his fingers, and Baron got up and moved inside. Jeremy followed slowly.

The main thing he noticed in Mr. Sherman's room were the big books everywhere. They were thicker than any books Jeremy had ever seen before. They filled a bookcase and were piled on tables and stacked on the floor. Jeremy had never known that one person could have so many books. Even their school didn't have this many.

"Sit down." Mr. Sherman took some books off a chair and put them on the floor.

Jeremy sat on the edge of one big chair, and Mr. Sherman sat in the other one. The dog went over and laid down at his feet.

"Now, where'd you come from, Jeremy?" Mr. Sherman scratched the dog's ears.

"Stony Crick, Kentucky."

"How'd you happen to come to Chicago?"

"We never would've, but our house burned down. Fenn had been tryin' to get Pa to come to Chicago for a long time anyhow. We're not really goin' to live here. We're just stayin' long enough to get money to go home and buy the store."

"I see. Well, Chicago probably looks pretty bad to you after the mountains. I came here from the country, too—a farm in Kansas."

"Do you live here all alone?"

"Except for Baron. How many brothers and sisters do you have?"

"Well, there's Ethan and Johnson, they're nine; and Caroline, she's six; and Homer D.'s seven."

"You'll all be going to school then, but you won't be in my class till you're in the sixth grade."

"We won't be here that long." Jeremy wasn't going to let anybody think that for a minute.

"Of course. I forgot."

Baron stretched and got to his feet, and Jeremy's fingers dug into the arm of his chair. Mr. Sherman said quietly, "Lie down, Baron," and he did.

"I never saw a dog that'd mind like that before," Jeremy said.

"Baron's a special dog. He's been trained to help me get around the city by myself. He lets me know when it's safe to cross the street and won't let me bump into people or fall over anything."

"What if he sees a cat?"

"As long as he has a harness on, he wouldn't even look at a cat."

Jeremy wished Baron had his harness on now. If what Mr. Sherman said was true, that dog was trained better than most young'uns, but just the same Jeremy didn't like the way he kept staring at him and running his tongue out like he was licking his chops.

Ever since he had come in, Jeremy'd been wondering what Mr. Sherman did with all those books since he couldn't see, but he didn't know whether it would be mannerly to ask. Finally he just had to.

"You have a lot of books," he began.

Mr. Sherman smiled. "Would you like to see one? Come over here to the table and I'll show you how I read with my fingers."

Baron lay halfway under that table, his bright eyes watching every move Jeremy made. Why had he asked about those fool books? That dog was just waiting for a good excuse to sink his teeth into him.

"Jeremy?" Ethan called outside the door. "You in there?" His voice had never sounded so good to Jeremy before.

Jeremy sprang off his chair. He wanted to get out of that room in a hurry, but he didn't want any more of Baron's attention than he already had. "I wish I could stay," he said, as he backed slowly toward the door, "but my brother's calling me." He really did want to see how Mr. Sherman read those books, but it made him feel better just to have the doorknob in his hand.

"Come back again," Mr. Sherman invited.

"I'd like to," Jeremy said, and he slipped quietly out into the hall.

"Where you been all this time?" Ethan asked. "You been gone an hour, and Ma's fit to be tied. Where's Caroline?"

Jeremy felt guilty. He'd forgotten all about Caroline. "She went to the store with Miz Quill." He hoped this was true.

"Then how come she isn't with her now?"

Jeremy looked down the street, and there came Mrs. Quill, taking small, precise steps and holding the hand of a thin, little girl with red hair and a pale face.

"Mr. Sherman was wrong." Jeremy hurried around the corner of the house before Mrs. Quill could focus her granite-colored stare on his dirty feet. Where could Caroline have got to? She might have tried to cross the street and got hit by a car. Or she might be lost. It would only take a few minutes for Caroline to get so lost in this place that they'd never see her again. He thought of Caroline's pretty, round face, her blue eyes brimming over with tears.

She was afraid of strangers. If she ever came back, he'd never tease her about anything again, and he'd see that Ethan and Johnson didn't either. He ran up the rickety stairs and into the dark apartment. He was thinking about Caroline so hard it seemed as if he could almost hear her singing in that soft, tuneless way she had. The door to the hall was open and now, besides Caroline singing, he could hear Ma laughing for the first time since they'd left home.

When he found Ma standing in the bathroom doorway, he could see what she was laughing about. There was Caroline sitting in the big white tub as grand as a queen, with all her clothes on. She had her head tilted to one side and one hand stuck out in front of her. She was staring at it with the same silly expression the lady on TV had when she was singing about the soap. She had the words too: "Clean and sweet from head to feet." The only thing was that Caroline's hand didn't look too clean and sweet; it was dirty.

Already he'd forgotten about his promise to himself. "You mean black as soot from head to foot," he teased. And Caroline began to cry. At least one thing was the same here as in Stony Crick.

# 5

## Bottom of the Box

"I need another bowl of grits, Ma," Ethan said. "You give me a mighty little one to start with."

"That's all there is," answered Ma. "We've got to the bottom of the box."

"Then why don't we get us another box?" Johnson asked. "The helpin's are gettin' littler every day."

"Maybe we don't have money enough for another box, stupid," Ethan told him.

"Watch who you're callin' stupid." Johnson flung his spoon across the table at Ethan.

Pa didn't even fault Johnson. His face got red, and he pushed his chair back and went out the door without saying a word. Ma just sat there listening to his footsteps as he went down the stairs.

"This just has to be the day Will finds another job," she said. "His spirit's bein' ground down further every day."

Ma wasn't looking at any of them. She must be praying, Jeremy thought. Ma always talked to God like she knew Him.

They'd been in Chicago a little more than three weeks, and Pa'd had one job and lost it already. Fenn hadn't told Pa how particular they were here about getting to work the very same minute every morning. It wasn't as if Pa'd been all that late. A couple of days it had been fifteen or twenty minutes, and the most he'd ever been late was half an hour, but at the end of the second week, they'd handed him his notice. Pa probably worked harder than anybody at that factory; it didn't seem fair to lose his job for such a picky little thing.

Jeremy pushed his chair back now. He didn't want to sit there and think about Pa with no job and maybe having to go on welfare. He hoped God had paid attention to Ma's prayer.

Last night after Ma and Pa thought everybody was asleep, he'd heard them talking louder than they ever had at home.

"If I'd wanted to go on welfare, I'd have stayed in Stony Crick," Pa'd said.

Jeremy'd tried to stop listening, but he just couldn't help it. Surely Ma didn't want them to go on welfare. Back home Pa'd said he'd eat tree bark before he'd even take any of the free government food that was passed out, let alone take any money.

But last night Ma'd said, "Pride's one thing and hungry kids is another. Tomorrow we'll use the last of the grits and next week the rent's due again. You know as well as I do that Miz Quill's not the kind that'll take kindly to waitin' for her money."

If Pa answered, Jeremy didn't hear what he said.

Jeremy looked out of the kitchen window into the dirty little alley. At Stony Crick they'd always hurried through breakfast so they could get outside, but here there wasn't any reason to hurry. Sometimes Ethan and Johnson went out and played in the alley, but he couldn't see much fun in kicking a tin can back and forth. He'd sooner stay in the house and try to teach Homer D. his ABC's.

All of a sudden there was a racket fit to raise the roof. There was hollering and calling back and forth and people stomping up and down the stairway inside the house.

"Sounds like the neighbors got back," Ethan said.

"Sounds more like an army." Ma was piling the dishes in the sink.

"Goody." Caroline ran toward the door. "I can't wait to see those six girls."

"I can," Ma said, but there was a little smile at the corners of her mouth.

"Some of them's out there in the hall right now." Caroline opened the door a crack and peeked through.

Before you could snap your fingers, the hall seemed to be full of girls, but when things quieted down enough to count them, there were just three. One of them had yellow hair like Caroline's. Two of them had black hair, and all of them had dirty faces.

"What's your name? Where'd you come from? How many kids you got? Got any cookies?" They all talked at once and didn't seem to expect any answers.

Then they were gone as fast as they had come, and so was Caroline. A wave of noise swept down the stairway and into the yard.

"I declare," Ma said, "it'll be like livin' with a tornado in the house."

Ethan and Johnson went out, too, but Jeremy stayed by the window. He tried not to see the dirty little yard. In his mind he was filling it with yellow-green popple trees and reddish-green oaks, with maybe here and there a dark pine or a shiny green holly, but it didn't work. That yard would never be anything but bare and ugly.

"Ma," he said, "don't you ever think about Stony Crick?"

"Seems like I don't think about hardly anythin' else. I can understand Lot's wife better every day, but I jist have to keep tellin' myself that it don't do no good to look back. Why don't you go on outside with the rest? You're gettin' as pale as a grub under a stone. Put your other shirt on, and I'll wash that one out."

At least the thought of washing something out seemed to make Ma some happier. Nobody dast lay anything down for a minute for fear Ma'd grab it up and stick it in the tub.

He was about to open the door when somebody started pounding on it from the other side. It was Mrs. Quill, and she was mad as a snapping turtle.

"Mrs. Weatherhead," she said, without first saying so much as good morning, "I couldn't believe it when Jean Elizabeth told me, but now I've seen it with my own eyes. Are you just throwing your garbage into my back yard?"

Ma's face reddened. "I supposed some creature'd come along and gobble it up in short order same as it would back home."

"Some creature like a rat," Mrs. Quill snapped. You'd better have a decent garbage can out there by tomorrow or I'll have the Board of Health on you."

She turned around and stalked out without another word. Ma was trying hard not to let her face crumple up like Caroline's.

"She talked like we was trash. It looks to me like them cans is overturned as much as they're upright." Ma sounded like Ethan trying to explain why he didn't do something he was supposed to do.

Jeremy slipped out of the door and started slowly down the rickety stairs, dragging one foot behind the other. Ma was always the one that knew what to do about everything. He couldn't bear to see her humbled because she hadn't caught on to all the Chicago ways yet. Who wanted to anyway? He bet Mrs. Quill would have a pretty hard time of it if she was all of a sudden to be set down in Stony Crick.

The other children were whooping and hollering up and down the alley, but he wanted to be left alone. He stuck close to the side of the house so nobody would notice him and started down the front walk. The sun felt good, but when he was walking along the street, he always felt as if there were dozens of eyes watching him. With so many windows in the tall buildings and so many cars driving past on the street, somebody must always be there to see every move anybody made. It made the hair on his head prickle.

And yet, if he really did meet anybody, they pretended they didn't even see him.

A black lady in a yellow dress came down the walk toward him now, a big bag of groceries in her arms. He said, "Howdy," and bobbed his head the way he'd been taught, but she grabbed her purse in both hands and scurried past him like she was afraid of him.

There were plenty of boys, black and white, living in the buildings up and down the street, but they stuck together in tight little bunches and didn't seem to hanker for anybody else's company. There was no making friends in Chicago even if you wanted to.

The cars going down the street were making such a racket and Jeremy was thinking so hard that he didn't know Mr. Sherman and Baron were walking behind him until they passed him on the sidewalk.

"Hi, Mr. Sherman," he said.

"Oh, it's Jeremy. Baron and I were out for our morning walk. Would you like to come along?"

"I'd be proud to." Jeremy circled cautiously around Baron, who was watching him carefully.

They walked briskly to the end of the block, and then turned down a quiet side street. This was farther than Jeremy had walked since they came.

"It's all the same, isn't it?" he asked.

"All what's the same?"

"The buildings and the streets and the sidewalks. In Stony Crick you can stand any place and it's different no matter which way you look. I wish you could see it." Jeremy stopped. What an unmannerly thing to say to a person who'd never see Stony Crick or anything else.

Mr. Sherman smiled. "I'd like to. What would you see if you stood in the door of your house in Stony Crick?"

"On a sunny day or a rainy day?"

"Let's try a rainy day."

"On a rainy day the first thing you'd notice would be the smells. If you had ten noses, you couldn't separate the smells all out. There's mint and catnip and pine and sassafras and just plain dirt and about a hundred other things. Blue Mountain looks smudgy in the rain, like somebody'd tried to erase it and almost got the job done."

"How about a sunny day?"

"The first thing you'd see if it was summer would be Ma's flowers. Ma's got flowers everywhere along the crick and in old tires and around the doorstep—" He thought of that doorstep the way it had looked the last time he saw it.

Mr. Sherman didn't press him to go on, and they walked along for a few minutes without saying anything, which was one of the good things about Mr. Sherman. He didn't think he had to chatter like a magpie every minute.

Finally, Mr. Sherman said, "I was homesick, too, when I first came to Chicago, but there are some good things here."

"What are they?"

"For one thing there's a lake as big as an ocean, with miles of beaches all around it. And you'll like the libraries and museums."

Jeremy couldn't imagine what a museum might be, but it sounded strange and exciting. And that lake must be something. Jeremy wondered if Pa and Ma knew about it.

An old house in the middle of the block was being torn down and Mr. Sherman wouldn't be able to see the little pile of bricks and lumber on the sidewalk just ahead of them.

"Stop!" Jeremy said. He grabbed Mr. Sherman's arm. "There's a pile of bricks ahead." Baron turned his head toward him, growling deep in his throat, and Jeremy felt cold all the way down to his toes.

"Quiet, boy! It's all right." Mr. Sherman's voice was firm. "Thanks, Jeremy. It's just that Baron doesn't take kindly to help."

"You mean he'd have kept you from falling over those bricks?"

"I'll show you."

Mr. Sherman backed up a few steps and said, "Forward!"

When Baron came to the bricks, he pushed against Mr. Sherman's leg until he'd nudged him away from the bricks and over to the curb.

"He's a heap smarter than I give him credit for," Jeremy had to admit. "I guess he'll do anything you tell him."

"Even better, a lot of times like this he tells me what to do."

Jeremy watched Baron all the way home. That dog was really smart. Once in a while a store front had a bright canvas awning sticking out several feet in front of the window. Mr. Sherman was tall enough to hit the awnings with his head, but every time they came to one of them, Baron led him safely around it. Jeremy didn't see how that dog knew about the awnings, because they were way over his head. Once when they started across the street, a car turned right in front of them. There wasn't time to step back on the curb, but the big dog put his body in front of Mr. Sherman and the car whizzed by, missing them by inches.

The sun was shining and the sky was blue, what you could see of it anyway. Jeremy liked to see a whole sky at once, though, not just a patch of it here and there. Still Chicago did seem a little better, as long as he was with Mr. Sherman.

When they got home, Homer D. was sitting on the bottom step, just rocking back and forth the way he liked to do. His face lit up when he saw Jeremy, and Jeremy sat down beside him. He intended to work on Homer D.'s ABC's every day till school started.

He fished around in his pocket and brought out a crumpled piece of paper and a pencil stub. When Homer D. saw the pencil, he squirmed and tried to stand up, but Jeremy pushed him back down.

"Now see here, Homer D., do you want to go to school or not? I promise not to get cross."

"Okay." Homer D. stopped wiggling and shifted closer to Jeremy.

"Now, what's this letter? We learned it yesterday."

Homer D. didn't say anything and Jeremy had to tell him. "It's an A."

Homer D. nodded. "An A," he said.

"See, I told you it was easy. This one's a B. Say B."

"B." Homer D. was grinning from ear to ear.

Jeremy showed him the A again. "What's this one?"

"Jeremy," Pa said. Jeremy didn't know he was there until he looked up and saw him.

Pa shook his head. "It's no use," he said sadly. "Why don't you let the boy be? It's not like anything could ever come of it."

Jeremy was sure Pa was wrong, but this was no time to argue with Pa about anything.

Just then Ma called down, "Will? Will, is that you?"

Pa started up the stairs. Jeremy tried to guess by the way he walked whether he had good news or bad, but he couldn't tell. He took Homer D.'s hand and they followed Pa upstairs. Even Homer D. walked a little faster than usual, as if he knew Jeremy was in a hurry.

Ma stood in the doorway, her cheeks pink and her hair damp, with comb marks still showing in it, like she'd freshened up just for Pa. She hadn't done that much lately.

"Well, Will?" she asked.

"Well, what?"

"Don't tease, Will. I can't stand it. Was Fenn right about the job or not?"

"Yep, there was a job all right." But Pa couldn't keep it up any longer. A little grin tugged at the corners of his mouth.

"You got it, Will. You got it!"

And Ma sat down in one of the red chairs and started to cry. There was no figuring Ma out any more. Those last few weeks when there'd really been something to worry about, Ma'd never cried a drop, and now when you'd think she'd be grinning from ear to ear, here she was bawling like Caroline.

But before supper was over, she'd really perked up and was making plans to go out next Saturday and buy them all shoes to start school with.

# 6

# "Leatherhead"

"Hurry up, Ethan!" Jeremy called up the stairway for the fifth time.

"Let's leave him," Johnson said. "Mr. Sherman's already turned the corner. We probably can't find him, and we'll get lost and miss the whole first day of school all on account of Ethan." Johnson's face was so scrubbed that his freckles looked as if they stood out from the rest of his face.

Caroline puckered up, but Jeremy told her, "Johnson's just foolin'. We'll get there all right."

Caroline really looked pretty today. Ma had tied a blue ribbon on each pigtail to match Caroline's new blue dress. The boys didn't have anything new except their shoes, but their jeans and faded, red plaid shirts were clean and ironed, and Jeremy guessed they all looked right nice for their first day of school.

Ethan came racing down the steps two at a time, and they all started after Mr. Sherman at a dead run. Just as

Caroline began to bawl that she had a pain in her side and they'd have to slow down, they saw Mr. Sherman up ahead. He waited for them when they hollered at him. Baron stood stiffly at his side, eyeing them all watchfully. He never wagged his tail like an ordinary dog.

They were several squares away from home, Jeremy proudly walking by Mr. Sherman's side while the others trailed behind, when Mr. Sherman asked, "You have your registration papers all right, don't you?" That stopped them dead in their tracks.

What with waiting for their turn in the bathroom and trying to help Ethan find his other shoe and Ma jawing at them about hurrying up and paying attention to the teacher and what she'd do if Johnson did any fighting, they'd walked off and left those fool papers right on the table.

"Will they really care if we don't have them?" Jeremy asked.

"I'm afraid they will," Mr. Sherman told him. "One of you'll have to go back for them. Jeremy, you've walked past the school with me several times, so you know the way. Why don't you go back, and the rest of you come on ahead with me? You'll be on time, Jeremy, if you hurry."

Caroline had hardly had time to unpucker. "I won't go without Jeremy," she said. "Ma told me to stay close to Jeremy." She grabbed onto him like a leech, and nothing they said could pry her loose.

"If Caroline's goin' back, we all will. We're not in such a swivet to get there anyhow," Ethan said, and he and Johnson trotted along behind Jeremy and Caroline.

When they'd finally got the papers and made it to the school, hot and out of breath, Ethan and Johnson were sure Jeremy'd made a mistake.

"That's a factory," Johnson said. "Whoever saw a school like that?"

"It is too a school," Jeremy insisted. "Mr. Sherman showed it to me twice already. How would you know what a school looks like in Chicago?"

He hadn't thought much of it, either, the first time he saw it, and he still didn't. The two-story, brick building was streaked with smoke, and a few windows on the first floor were boarded up. There wasn't a blade of grass or a tree or a bush in sight, and the playground was covered with some kind of rock and had a high chain link fence all the way around it, like a prison. There wasn't any fence around the Stony Crick school. When it was recess, you could go wherever you had a mind to—into the weeds to pick hickory nuts or down to the crick to cool off your feet. And their feet were going to need a sight more cooling off here than they had at home, what with the rock on the playground and their tight new shoes.

They must be the very last ones to get to school. There wasn't another soul on the sidewalk in front of the building or on the wide stone steps leading up to the big double doors.

It was even worse inside than out. The doors opened into a long hall that was dark and gloomy in spite of the lights that shone down from the high, white ceilings. There was a closed-in smell of dust and soap and sweat.

There was a long table against one wall, with three women and a man who looked cross as two sticks sitting behind it, sorting through stacks of papers. They all looked tired and hot, even though it was early morning.

The Weatherheads inched up to the table, walking as close together as they could. Jeremy handed their papers to one of the women at the table. After she read through

*44*

them, she looked up and smiled. Then she wrote out four cards and handed them to a tall, dark-haired girl standing by the table.

"Gertie will take you to your rooms," she said.

Rooms? For the first time Jeremy realized that in a big school like this they'd all be in different places. He tried to imagine a schoolroom where he couldn't look across and see Ethan's dark head bent over a reader or Johnson making spitballs behind his geography book.

They turned down another hall, still bunched together so close they were stepping on each other. Caroline still hung onto Jeremy's hand. Johnson didn't even say anything when Ethan stepped on his feet; Jeremy'd never seen him look so cowed.

Gertie stopped in front of an open door.

"This is the first grade," she said, looking at Caroline. Caroline didn't take a step toward the room; she didn't even let go of Jeremy's hand. He didn't know what to do. He didn't want to shove her into the room; for one thing she'd holler if he did.

Just when it looked like he'd have to stand there all day with Caroline stuck to him like a cocklebur, a pretty teacher, wearing a blue dress and shoes to match, came to the door. She smiled at Caroline and said, "We really need a girl in here; this year there are mostly boys. I like the way the bows on your hair match your eyes."

She held out her hand, and Caroline took it. She touched one of her bows with her other hand and walked off without so much as looking back.

When the door closed behind them, Jeremy was glad she hadn't cried, but couldn't help wishing she'd looked like she was going to miss him some.

The boys followed Gertie up a broad stairway with a

railing down the middle. Ethan and Johnson were in the same room right at the head of the stairs. Jeremy had never felt so lonesome as when the door closed behind the two of them. They didn't look back, either.

Gertie turned another corner, and pointed down another long hall. "Room seventeen's down there," she said. "Your teacher's Mrs. McNutt."

Jeremy walked as slowly as he dared, but he couldn't put off getting to room seventeen forever. There it was, the door solid and closed in front of him. Would it be unmannerly to open it and walk in, or should he knock? He took hold of the big brass doorknob and then raised his hand and knocked instead. Nothing happened, so he turned the knob. At the same time the door opened from the other side, and Jeremy, thrown off balance, lurched into the room. It seemed like a hundred pairs of eyes, some in black faces and some in white, stared at him, and a hundred throats laughed. The tall woman who had opened the door looked at him out of cold gray eyes and held out her hand. Jeremy stuck his out to shake hands the way he'd been taught. Now the laughter was a roar.

"Give me your card. You're late," the teacher said crisply.

Jeremy's face turned red as he realized that she hadn't meant to shake hands with him at all; she only wanted his card.

"Jeremy Weatherhead," she read out loud. "From Kentucky. Well, Jeremy Weatherhead, you're lucky; there's a seat left for you. But if more of you keep coming up here, I don't know where we're going to put you all."

Jeremy started for the empty seat, feeling unwanted. It certainly hadn't been his idea to come.

When he was halfway up the aisle, he saw too late that a

bucktoothed, red-headed boy had stuck his foot out faster than a snake. Jeremy tried to save himself, but it was too late. He stumbled and sprawled across the desk of a dark-skinned girl who drew back and said, "Ugh!"

Now they all laughed fit to kill again. They kept it up until the teacher knocked on her desk and said, "That will be enough."

Things did quiet down then till a skinny, yellow-haired boy, sitting over by the window, whispered, "Jeremy Weatherhead fell on his leather head." And that started them off again. Jeremy just slunk into his seat and didn't look at anyone. If he were more like Johnson, he'd have lit into that boy and shaken some of the meanness out. He wondered how Johnson was getting along. Ma'd said she'd beat the tar out of him if he did any fighting the first day.

Jeremy thought about the time Johnson had taken on three boys at once and pretty near whipped them all before the teacher got outside and doused the four of them with a bucket of water.

All of a sudden there was an almighty racket out in the hall, and Jeremy jumped clean out of his seat and into the aisle. That set them all to laughing again.

"Didn't you ever hear a recess bell before?" somebody asked.

As a matter of fact, Jeremy never had. Their teacher at Stony Crick had been satisfied just to tell them it was time to go out; she didn't see any call to scare them all half to death.

He followed the rest out to the playground. They had to march out in a line here; they weren't supposed to cut and run the way they did at home. No hollering either; it just wasn't natural.

As soon as they got out, they began choosing up sides for a ball game. One captain was the red-headed boy who had tripped him up in the schoolroom. His name was Nick. The other captain was the skinny boy who had made sport of Jeremy's name. His name was Joe, and Jeremy could see it was going to be uphill work to find anything good about either one of them, in spite of Ma's always saying there was something good in everybody.

By the time they got down about twenty names, Jeremy decided not to hang around any more. They probably weren't going to choose him at all. Even if they did, he'd be the last one, and he was darned if he was going to be the old cow's tail.

There were some smaller kids playing at the other end of the playground. Maybe he could find Ethan and Johnson. He looked quite a while before he saw a red head next to a black one in a big circle where they were playing dodge ball. Jeremy ran over; they'd really be glad to see him.

"Hey!" he called out. "Hey, Ethan!" But a skinny little black girl in a yellow dress was in the center, really dodging that ball, first on one foot and then on the other, and everybody was hollering and jumping up and down and clapping hands.

"Johnson?" he called out, but Ethan and Johnson were having a high old time. They didn't hear him, and they didn't seem to be missing him any.

He went over and looked through the fence at the traffic going by in the street. He probably wouldn't have liked to play on that rock anyway; he'd rather have good old dirt under his feet. Lots of times he was the first one chosen in Stony Crick.

48

The rest of the morning dragged by till finally it was time for lunch.

Mrs. McNutt said, "As you know, in our school this year we are going to try having hot lunches at noon instead of bringing our lunches or going home. You are very fortunate; this is an experimental program, and you will not need to bring any money this week. Listen carefully; I will tell you this only once."

"You will follow me to the cafeteria two-by-two. There will be no unnecessary noise. In the cafeteria you will each take a tray and your silverware, which will be wrapped up in your napkin. Food will be put on your plates. You will be shown where to sit, and you will eat in the same place every day. You are not to dawdle, but you are expected to clean your plates. When you are through, you will be shown what to do with your dishes. Then you will go to the playground until the bell rings."

Mrs. McNutt went to the door at the back of the room. There was a quick scrambling, and then everybody had a partner but Jeremy. He trailed the others down to the basement, which had gray-painted walls and smelled like steam and strange food and too many people in one place.

In the cafeteria line a white-haired lady with a white cap on her head picked up a plate, plopped a huge spoonful of some kind of mess on it and handed it to another lady, who added a slippery peach with some lumpy white stuff on it and handed it to Jeremy. He hoped he could get it down because Mrs. McNutt expected him to, but he wasn't hungry. He even thought he might be sick. His place was between two girls. One of them was the girl whose desk he'd fallen on; the other one wasn't even in his room. Neither of them looked at him, and he didn't look at them after he sat down.

The worst thing on his plate was that peach and

*50*

whatever was on top of it. Only the thought of Mrs. McNutt's face made him swallow any of it after the first mouthful; he could feel those lumps all the way down. He chased that fool peach all over his plate with his fork and spoon both. All of a sudden it shot clean off his plate and landed in the lap of the girl he'd not seen before. She squealed like a pig caught under a gate and jumped out of her seat. That gave Jeremy such a start, he knocked his milk over on the girl on the other side.

"You really are a— Leatherhead!" she hollered. There was quite a commotion before everything was cleaned up.

The afternoon seemed almighty long, but at least nobody took any particular notice of him.

Ethan and Johnson were full of talk on the way home after school. Ethan had stayed in the center in the ball game longer than anyone, and Johnson hadn't felt any call to fight all day. Ma ought to be happy about that.

Caroline limped along crying because her new shoes made her feet hurt.

"Then why don't you take them off?" Ethan asked.

She did, and before they got home she was chattering along a mile a minute about her new teacher.

Jean Elizabeth Quill had got home ahead of them and was sitting on the front steps.

"You're barefooted," she said accusingly.

"I know it." Caroline was wiggling her bare toes.

"Her new shoes hurt," Ethan explained.

"Do you want to come up and play?" Caroline asked Jean Elizabeth.

"I guess so."

Jean Elizabeth followed Caroline upstairs, but she didn't work out to be a whole lot of company.

"You want to play house?" Caroline asked.

"I don't care."

"Want a cooky?"

"I don't care."

"Want to play ball?"

"I don't care."

Before they could find something Jean Elizabeth did care about, her mother called out, "Jean Elizabeth, are you upstairs? You come home this minute."

"See if you can come back," Caroline coaxed her, but she never did.

# 7

---

# Fire!

"The huntin' season was plumb near over the day I got shot at." They were all really listening now. This was the first time Jeremy'd stood up in front of the class to give an oral report without wanting to sink through the floor. And then Mrs. McNutt had to go and spoil it.

"The huntin' season was almost over. It was a right foggy morning, and first thing Pa flew off the handle because—"

"My father was angry because—"

Jeremy tried to think of Pa as "my father." Mrs. McNutt and the class were waiting. "My father was angry because I'd left the ax in the woods. He said it was probably up to its midsides in water." He looked quickly at Mrs. McNutt and went on. "If it hadn't been for the fog I might could have—"

"I probably could have—"

"I probably could have brung it—"

"I probably could have brought it—"

Jeremy sighed. Trying to tell a story with Mrs. McNutt on his back was like trying to make water run uphill. He hurried through the rest of the story as fast as he could. If he could tell it his own way, he could have them feeling that bullet whizzing through their hats. And they'd have laughed when he told how he raised up to show he wasn't a squirrel and got another hole plugged in his hat. As it was he just said he got shot at and sat down. It wasn't much of a story.

Talking about Stony Crick got Jeremy to thinking about it, and he hardly listened while the others droned on about going to the Museum of Natural History and getting lost in department stores and having their tonsils out. The subject today was "An Exciting Adventure."

Mrs. McNutt talked, too, but he didn't listen to her, either. He was listening to the wind rustling in the oak trees back home. All of a sudden the bell he'd never gotten used to clanged louder than it ever had before. Everyone was getting out of their seats, and he heard somebody say, "Fire drill."

Fire! They were going to have to hurry a whole lot faster than they were if they were going to get out of the school alive. He didn't even have to close his eyes to see the flames shooting out of the roof of their house on that awful night. They'd been asleep just minutes before.

"Hurry up!" he hollered. "Run, before the whole thing goes up!"

They just looked at him as though they were deaf and went on taking partners like they weren't any more than going to lunch. Most of them laughed, and Mrs. McNutt gabbled something at him, but he didn't wait to find out what it was.

He ran out into the hall. There were teachers and kids

coming out of doors all up and down the hall, moving as leisurely as if they didn't have any more on their minds than a game of dodge ball. "Run!" he hollered, squeezing past the crowd on the stairway. "She'll cave in before you know it!"

They all gave Jeremy the same blank look he'd gotten in his own room. Some of them hollered at him and tried to grab his arm, but he didn't pay any attention. He had to get down the stairs to Caroline. Ever since their fire even a lighted match could scare her into fits.

But on the first floor Caroline's room was empty. It seemed to Jeremy that her teacher had more sense than the rest.

Now the halls were full of people. They were walking pretty fast, but if there was much of a fire they'd never all get out at the rate they were going. "Run," he kept hollering. "Run!"

Then he felt a firm hand on his shoulder and heard Mr. Sherman's quiet voice.

"Slow down, Jeremy," he said. "This isn't a real fire; it's just a practice."

"A practice fire? Who'd do a fool thing like that?"

"It's not such a bad idea, really. If this many people all tried to run out of the building at the same time, we'd all end up with broken legs, so we practice getting out as fast as we can without running and falling over each other. Didn't your teacher explain about the fire drill beforehand?"

It was a good thing Mr. Sherman followed his class outside without waiting for an answer, because Jeremy hated to tell him he didn't know whether she had or not. That last five or ten minutes when Mrs. McNutt had been chattering on while he was thinking about Stony Crick she could have been talking about almost anything. Wouldn't you know? The first worthwhile thing she'd said all day, and he hadn't been listening. Now he'd made a fool of himself again.

He'd never go back to that room. He couldn't. With all this hoopla going on he could head for home and nobody'd even miss him. The bell rang again and everyone started pouring back into the building. He made for the closest door. His head down so he wouldn't have to look at anybody, he whirled around and bumped spang into Mr. Sherman.

"Where are you going?" Mr. Sherman asked.

"Home," Jeremy mumbled.

"Oh, it's you, Jeremy. Why are you— Don't worry about what happened. Everybody makes mistakes."

"Nowhere near as many as I do," Jeremy said.

"Tell you what—suppose I go back up with you and talk to Mrs. McNutt. I've already talked to Mr. Harper, the principal, and you're not in any trouble."

Mr. Sherman kept a firm grip on Jeremy's shoulder, but Jeremy knew he'd be wasting his breath trying to talk Mrs. McNutt into thinking Jeremy wasn't a fool. Or making anybody else think so, for that matter.

He was right. Every time anybody looked at him all the rest of the day, they burst out laughing. It seemed like three o'clock would never come. Usually he kept his eye peeled for Ethan and Johnson and walked home with them, but today he didn't see hide nor hair of either one of them.

When he got home, he noticed the Buckhorn girls all in a circle, playing some kind of a game out on the sidewalk by the steps. They were all laughing and giggling; at least somebody was having fun. When he got close enough to

56

see what they were doing, it really got his dander up. They were all prancing around in a circle with their toes turned in and their elbows stuck out. There in the center of the circle was Homer D., grinning from ear to ear. He didn't even know they were making sport of him, but Jeremy did.

"Homer D.," he said crossly, "you come right out of there."

"Out of there," Homer D. said, but he didn't move out of the circle. He was having a high old time. He didn't know they were making fun of him.

"Out of there, out of there," the Buckhorns echoed. Jeremy clenched his fists. Why did the Buckhorns have to be girls?

He grabbed Homer D. and jerked him over to the stairs. Homer D. started to beller, and Ma popped her head out of the door.

Before she could say anything Ethan and Johnson hove into sight. Johnson's shirt was torn, and one of his eyes was almost swelled shut.

"Johnson Weatherhead, you come up here this minute," Ma said. "I told you what would happen if you got into any fights at school."

"But I had to, Ma. I had to this time."

Ethan was climbing the stairs behind Johnson. "He did have to, Ma. They was all making fun of us on account of the dumb thing Jeremy done. We had a fire drill, and that Jeremy run through the halls hollerin' and carryin' on, and—"

The door closed behind them, and Jeremy dropped down on the bottom step, feeling sick. Homer D. sat down and snuggled up to him. Jeremy guessed Homer D. was the only one in the world who wasn't going to make fun of him.

Caroline came along, out of breath like always. She squeezed in on the other side of Homer D. "You should have seen Miss Evans today. She had the prettiest pink dress on. She has a new one almost every day. I wish Ma had a pink dress like that."

At least as long as she was jabbering about her teacher, she wasn't talking about the fire drill. Maybe Caroline didn't even know what happened. She always changed subjects so fast it was hard to keep up with her. Now she was wishing they had curtains at the windows and a tablecloth like the Quills. Caroline had only been in the Quills' house once for a few minutes, but she must have learned everything in it by heart because she was always wishing they had something the Quills had.

It seemed as if Caroline wished for a mighty sight of things these days anyhow, generally things like pink dresses and tablecloths. There was only one thing Jeremy wished for, and that was to be home where nobody gave much thought to things like that, not even Caroline.

When they got upstairs, Caroline said, "Can I ask Jean Elizabeth to play?"

"I don't know's I would." Ma's lips tightened.

"Why not, Ma?"

"I just wouldn't; that's all."

"Every blessed time she gets anywhere near here, her mother hollers for her to come home anyhow," Ethan said.

"That's what I meant," Ma said.

That night at supper every one of them was crosser than a bee-stung bear. It started with Ethan spilling his milk in Johnson's lap.

Johnson was all ready to wade into Ethan, but Ma

jumped first. "Can't you be more careful? Spillin' milk's just like spillin' money. And land knows we don't have much of it to spill."

That got Pa's dander up. "Don't you fault me on not havin' enough money. I near broke my back today loadin' fifty-pound boxes onto a truck. I can't do no more than to work from sunup to sundown."

"I never said you could. I just said there's not much money and there isn't."

"Since when isn't eighty dollars a week much money?"

"In Stony Crick it would be, but when you pay out thirty dollars for rent every blessed week and pay double what it costs at home for food, there's not much left for throwin' around. To say nothin' of buyin' shirts for boys to tear up in fights."

"I told you I had to fight on account of Jeremy."

Ma looked at Jeremy. "I didn't hear yet how you come to raise such a ruckus at the school."

Jeremy kept his eyes on his plate. "I don't want to talk about it."

"Your Ma asked you a question." Pa didn't use that tone of voice very often.

For some reason Caroline picked this moment to ask, "Why can't we have us some curtains at our windows like the Quills?"

"Dumbhead," Ethan said, "because we don't have no money."

"Don't ever let me hear you call your sister that again," Pa ordered.

At least they'd got away from the subject of school. There was more arguing, but Jeremy closed his ears to it. They never used to argue and pick at each other like this at home. They'd had other things to set their tongues to—news about neighbors and talk about hunting and crops and fishing.

Jeremy tried to remember the feel of a big old catfish tugging at his line till his pole quivered in his hands. And he could taste that fish, fried crisp in cornmeal batter. The only fish they'd had in Chicago didn't have any taste to it at all.

Jeremy felt like a rabbit caught in a trap. He had to get out of this stuffy little room so full of cross voices and the smell of stale food. Maybe if he had some fresh air, he'd get over feeling that every one of them was different than the way they'd been before. They'd never had much money at Stony Crick, but he'd never heard Pa and Ma fault each other about it before.

He pushed back his chair and opened the door to the stairway. As soon as he stepped outside, a curtain of rain blew into his face. It might've been raining all the while they were eating and they wouldn't even know it.

# 8

## Nick Calls the Tune

"Ma, where's my clean shirt?" Jeremy stuck his head through the kitchen doorway.

"Put on the one you wore yesterday." Ma was frying potatoes for breakfast again and didn't even turn around.

Ma sure had changed. He'd worn that shirt for three days now, and there was a big grease spot right in the front from yesterday morning's potatoes.

He could hear Ethan pounding on the bathroom door. "You going to be in there all day? Every last one of us'll be late for school."

Jeremy rummaged through the dirty-clothes bag and found a shirt that didn't have a grease spot in the front.

Pa'd lost the job he had when school started, but he had day work most of the time. They hadn't had to go on welfare or borrow anything from Fenn, but it was October now and they were a long way from having very much saved up to go back home.

Jeremy sat down at the table and picked with his fork at

the greasy potatoes on his plate. He was glad Ma didn't pay much attention any more as to whether they cleaned their plates or not. He took a swallow of milk and almost spit it out. He wished Mrs. Quill had never told Ma about powdered milk being cheaper. Ethan and Caroline didn't mind it, but he and Johnson couldn't stomach it. Ma said the other kind of milk wouldn't keep in this weather anyhow without an icebox. No matter how hot it was outdoors at home in Stony Crick, the milk and butter were always cool and fresh in the springhouse Pa'd built over the crick.

Ethan and Johnson dashed off early. It was their turn to feed the rabbit in their schoolroom and clean his cage.

Caroline's friends Stella and Cora Sue stopped at the bottom of the steps and hollered, "Caroline!"

Jeremy waited a while for the last of the Buckhorns to get clear of the bathroom. He wasn't in too much of a hurry; there·wasn't anyone waiting for him. The boys and Caroline seemed to make friends as easy as falling off a log. That just left Homer D. for Jeremy, and after a while he wasn't much company.

When Jeremy got to the bottom of the steps, he realized that it was too quiet. If he didn't hurry, Mrs. McNutt would be hopping mad. He'd been late twice this week already.

He slid into his seat just before the bell rang. Nobody so much as looked at him as far as he could tell. They didn't laugh at him much any more, but he didn't know but what he liked it better when they did. At least that showed they knew he was there.

While Mrs. McNutt was writing the math problems on the board, Darlene Baker, who sat in front of him, turned around and looked at him. Jeremy smiled at her; Darlene had never said a word to him since he came. And she wasn't going to now. She held onto her nose with one hand and fanned the air daintily with the other one. Then she turned around to bend over the math problems on her desk. Jeremy's face was red. Maybe he was a hillbilly, but he wasn't dirty. Then he looked down at his shirt, rumpled from two days in the dirty-clothes sack. And it didn't smell too good; it sure as anything didn't. He used to think he could do without Ma grabbing his clothes to wash every time she had a chance, but at least nobody'd ever had to hold their nose at him before. It was Friday; maybe tomorrow he could help Ma wash. He might even help her clean the windows. Most days now when they got home from school, Ma was just sitting there looking out of the window with her hands in her lap. He couldn't ever remember seeing Ma with her hands quiet before they came to Chicago.

After school Nick strutted up to him, grinning with his buckteeth like a hound that'd cornered a possum. "What do you know?" he asked.

Jeremy backed off a little and didn't answer. Nick wanted him to say "nothing," but he was darned if he would.

"How'd you like to go to the park with us tomorrow?" Nick asked. "It's Saturday," he added.

Jeremy didn't trust Nick, but Pa always said you'd ought to meet a person halfway. "Sure, I reckon."

"See you outside the store about eleven, then."

"What store?" Jeremy asked.

"The big one across from the park."

"What for?"

"You'll see. Just be there." And Nick strutted off.

Jeremy still didn't really like Nick, but it seemed that

any friend would be better than none. Maybe this would be the last time he had to walk home alone.

He could see Mr. Sherman and Baron about a block ahead, and he ran to catch up with them.

The three of them walked along for a while in companionable silence. When they got to the straggly little tree at the corner of Mrs. Quill's yard, Mr. Sherman asked, "Are the leaves beginning to turn?"

"No, they just look kind of dry and dusty," Jeremy said. "You'd ought to see Stony Crick in the fall. The sweet gums are the best; they turn every color from yellow to purple."

He closed his eyes and tried to really see Stony Crick in the fall, but it didn't seem so clear any more—more like a dream he'd had or a picture he'd seen someplace. But he wouldn't let himself get like Ethan and Johnson and not care whether he went home or not; he wouldn't.

He left Mr. Sherman at the porch, and ran up the stairs two at a time. "Ma!" he called the minute he burst into the kitchen. "Ma! Why can't we go home right now and not wait to make all that money to buy the store? The neighbors said they'd help us raise a house, and we don't need a store."

Ma was sitting in a chair by the table, and for a minute she sat up straight and looked at him with her eyes shiny like they used to be. Then she turned away from him and looked at the window. "You know we can't do that. It's not sensible."

Of course Jeremy knew they couldn't. He didn't know what had got into him.

He was waiting outside the market the next morning when Nick and Joe came along.

"Since you're new, we're gonna let you be the lucky one," Nick told him.

"Lucky how?" Jeremy still didn't really trust Nick.

"You get to lift the meat."

"Lift what meat?"

Nick and Joe laughed. "We take turns swiping lunch meat. There's nothing to it."

"You mean stealing?"

"It's not really stealing. A big store like that has so much money, they don't care about a little lunch meat."

"No, sir; I'm not stealing nothing from nobody."

"What did I tell you?" Joe said. "I knew he'd chicken out. Let's go." And Nick and Joe started down the street. They didn't even look back.

Jeremy didn't know what came over him, but he'd never felt so left out before. All of a sudden he knew he'd cross the deepest river on a rotten rail just to have one friend, let alone two.

"Hey," he called out, "I'll do it."

First he thought they didn't hear. Then they turned around and came back, grinning.

"Okay," Joe said, "here's what you do." He gave Jeremy a nickel to buy a candy bar with. He said when Jeremy went past the checker, she'd look at the candy bar and the nickel and wouldn't know there were two or three packages of lunch meat inside his shirt.

His legs felt like two sticks of wood when he pushed that door open. He'd only been in the market a couple of times before, and then Ma and Caroline and Ethan and Johnson had been along. And he hadn't been planning to do any stealing.

Stealing? All of a sudden he felt like he'd swallowed something he couldn't get down. He turned around, but there were those two pairs of eyes staring at him from the other side of the window. He stiffened his back and started down the aisle. Before, he'd liked the way the store smelled—like coffee and soap and oranges. This time the smells made him feel sick.

There were a lot of people in the store, but they were all busy filling their carts with things from the shelves. He wondered what it would be like to push a cart up and down the aisles, putting in whatever he wanted. Maybe Caroline's and Homer D.'s faces wouldn't light up when they saw the pickles and cookies and canned peaches, though.

For a minute he almost forgot why he was there. Then he remembered, and his heart began to bang against his chest so hard he was surprised nobody turned around to look.

Where was the meat in this store anyhow? He walked up and down, past the sugar and the flour and the crackers and the soup. And there was the meat counter, stretched all the way across the back of the store. He walked slower and slower, but the first thing he knew, there he was staring down at the chickens and the pork chops and the bacon. Maybe they'd be out of lunch meat today. He tried not to see it, but at the end of the case were stacks and stacks of lunch meat all wrapped up in little packages.

There were lots of people at the meat counter, too, but still nobody looked at him even once. He stood there for a while, just looking at those little packages of meat. Then he reached out his hand; it was shaking just like Grandpa's used to do after he'd turned eighty. This isn't stealing, he thought, not like stealing from a person. He touched a package, and then he saw a hand next to his. A lady with a baby in the back of her shopping cart picked up two packages and went on past without even glancing at him. He looked all around. Now there wasn't anyone anywhere near him. He reached out again. This time he grabbed three packages and stuffed them into the front of his shirt. He hoped Ma'd sewed the buttons on good.

Now all he had to do was get a candy bar and pay for it and get out of the store. His face felt wet and sticky even though the store was cool.

He looked out of the window and stopped right where he was. There, coming along the walk toward the store, was Ma, dragging Homer D. along. That was bad enough, but what was worse, right behind them were Nick and Joe, trying to walk like Homer D. They toed in and let their arms hang out funny and had their heads drooped over to one side. Joe even had his tongue lolling out of his mouth. That made Jeremy see red. Maybe Homer D. couldn't walk or talk so good, but they didn't have any call to make sport of him. Leastways he never did anything mean in his life, and he never tried to get anybody else to. Right then Jeremy knew what he had to do.

He headed straight back for the meat counter. All of a sudden that meat in his shirt seemed to weigh almighty heavy. The sweat poured down his face like spring rain, just thinking about what he'd almost done. Anybody that thinks it's hard to pick up a couple of packages of meat and stuff them inside a shirt ought to try getting them back out again, he thought. Ma was going to wonder why he only had one button left on his shirt.

He was putting the meat down where it belonged when somebody clapped a hand on his shoulder.

"I want to talk to you."

He looked up, and there was a black man in a white shirt and black tie, looking about seven feet tall. He was the blackest man Jeremy had seen yet, as black as a moonless night. Jeremy couldn't tell anything about his expression. He didn't look cross, but he wasn't smiling either.

"Come back to my office," the man said. He didn't let go of Jeremy's shoulder, and Jeremy had to take big steps and try to hold his shirt shut with one hand. He hoped Ma and Homer D. didn't see him; he felt bad enough without that.

The office was a little room at the back of the store. The man sat down at a big desk all covered with papers and told Jeremy to sit down across from him. That was a good thing, because his knees wouldn't have held him up much longer.

The man pushed some papers back and forth on his desk for a while and didn't say a word. A little sign on his desk said, "Mr. Garfield, Store Manager." Jeremy began to wonder if Mr. Garfield remembered he was there. Then the man looked up.

"Why did you do it?" he asked.

Jeremy sat there trying to figure out what to say.

Before he had it whipped, Mr. Garfield said, "I don't mean why did you take the meat; I mean why did you put it back?"

Ma always said, "Tell the truth and shame the devil," and the first thing Jeremy knew he'd told the whole story. He'd never had the chance to talk so long before without somebody breaking in.

Mr. Garfield never said a word the whole time he was talking. Once somebody came to the door, and he told them he was busy and they'd have to come back later.

When Jeremy finally got to the end, Mr. Garfield said, "Why do you think you were picked for this job?"

All of a sudden Jeremy realized he'd been dumber than

Homer D. Nick and Joe didn't want to be friends. They didn't even want the lunch meat. They just wanted to get him in trouble. Maybe Leatherhead was the right name for him—not to see through those two.

"They knew I'd get caught and wanted me to be in trouble," he said.

"I used to see Nick and Joe in here quite a bit before I got the mirrors set up," Mr. Garfield told him.

He could see Jeremy didn't know what he was talking about, so he took him out in the store and showed him the big mirrors over some of the counters. Sure enough, in these mirrors you could see what people were doing clear across the store. He could see Ma and Homer D. in one of them, just going out the door.

Jeremy and Mr. Garfield went back to the office. Mr. Garfield told him that two or three times when he'd caught boys stealing, he'd seen Joe and Nick standing around just outside.

Jeremy began to think he wasn't the first one they'd talked into trouble. And he began to wonder how they could have got him so mixed up. Even if that meat was bought by a big company, he didn't have any more right to steal from it than from his next-door neighbor.

Mr. Garfield asked a lot of questions and made Jeremy promise to bring Pa in to see him first thing Monday morning. "It's a school holiday, so you'll be able to come," Mr. Garfield told him.

Jeremy didn't sleep much that night, nor the next, for thinking what Pa would say when Mr. Garfield told him what had happened.

# 9

## The Monster

Jeremy tiptoed out to look at the clock on the kitchen shelf. Three o'clock. The last time he'd looked it had been a quarter after two. He couldn't count on Ma and Pa staying in bed more than about four more hours.

He'd had an awful time last night trying to figure out how to tell Pa that Mr. Garfield wanted to see him. He couldn't tell them what really happened Saturday and he couldn't lie to them; he just couldn't. Finally he'd told them that somebody at school had given him a nickel for a candy bar and while he was in the store he'd got acquainted with the manager and the manager said he wanted to talk to Pa. Right away they'd asked if he was in some kind of trouble, and while he didn't lie, he kind of talked around the truth by saying, "Why would I be in trouble for buying a candy bar?" That had satisfied them, though Ma'd faulted him for taking money that he couldn't pay back.

Jeremy couldn't swallow a mouthful at breakfast, but Ma'd perked up a little.

"Will," she said, "maybe that manager wants to give you a steady job." She didn't even notice that she'd given Johnson two bowls of mush.

"Jobs ain't all that easy to come by," Pa told her. But he sounded a little like he thought Ma might be right.

How Jeremy wished that was what Mr. Garfield was going to do instead of shaming him before Pa. To start with, he hadn't seemed to be the kind of man who would want to do that. But at least he hadn't called a policeman. Jeremy guessed he'd ought to be thankful for that.

It had always seemed like quite a way to the store before, but this morning it popped up almost as soon as they got out on the sidewalk.

Jeremy looked up at Pa. "Mr. Garfield's a black man," he said, not really knowing why he thought he had to explain.

Pa looked at him levelly. "So he's black," he said. "Is that supposed to matter?"

"No," Jeremy admitted, and he led Pa back to the office, trying not to look at the meat counter. The door was closed; maybe Mr. Garfield wouldn't be there. But before Jeremy could decide whether they ought to knock or not, the door opened and a white-jacketed clerk came out. Mr. Garfield looked up from his desk and saw Jeremy and Pa standing there. He motioned for them to come in.

Mr. Garfield smiled at Pa. "I'm sure Jeremy told you I wanted to talk to you about a job," he said.

Jeremy's knees felt weak. He was sure Mr. Garfield hadn't said anything about a job before, but now he was saying, "When I was questioning Jeremy on Saturday, he told me you were good with motors, and it just happens that my brother-in-law's in a spot right now where he needs a man who's good with a motor. You've probably noticed Keller's Filling Station down in the next block.

Well, Pete Keller's my brother-in-law. He's laid up; the doctor says he can't get back to work for a month or more, and not one of the boys at the station knows anything more than how to pump gas. Pete's left it up to me to find someone, and I was just about to give up."

He and Pa talked for quite a spell, and it ended with his telling Pa to go over to the filling station and ask for Walt. He never even opened his mouth about Jeremy and the meat.

Jeremy must've passed Keller's Filling Station a hundred times; he usually stopped to watch for a few minutes because there was always something interesting going on. He never would have dreamed that some day his own father would be working there. Maybe he'd even have a blue uniform with his name on the pocket like the rest of the men he'd seen changing tires and pumping gas.

He hoped Pa would let him go along to the station, but when they left the store Pa said, "Ma'll be frettin' to hear the news. Tell her I don't know whether I'll be home for dinner or not." He sounded more like the old Pa.

"How do you think you'll like workin' for a black man?" Ma asked Pa when he got home that night.

"I'm ashamed of you, Harriet," Pa answered. "Did you think I was just talkin' that first day when I told the boys it's what's under the skin that counts? They took to the idea with no problem; I never thought you'd be the one to give me trouble."

Ma looked ashamed. "I know, Will. I know you're right. It's just that some things take a little gettin' used to. That Mr. Garfield sounds like a mighty nice man, and his brother must be, too."

Ma really perked up after that October morning. The

windows shone so you could see your face in them, and you had to hang onto your clothes to keep them out of the washtub.

Pa took to that job like a duck to water.

Mr. Keller was gone for several weeks, and Pa was really on pins and needles the day they expected him back.

"I guess this is the day I kiss my job good-by," he said when he left in the morning.

But when he came home that night, Ma and Jeremy could tell just by the way he walked that everything was all right. He hugged Ma, pleased as punch.

"Bet you was never hugged by a genuwine, full-fledged mechanic before," he told her. "I was nervous as a long-tailed cat in a room full of rockin' chairs with Mr. Keller hangin' over my shoulder all morning. But when he finally called me over to talk to him, I tried to act like bein' fired wouldn't make no difference. Then he said he couldn't afford to lose a man like me—that I wouldn't do nothin' but work on motors from now on, and my pay would go up fifty cents an hour."

"Oh, Will," Ma said, "it's like a miracle. Especially since you'd rather fix cars than eat."

"The good part is," Pa said, "that now we can do both."

Since then Ma'd been able to set a little aside out of each pay check. It looked like they'd get back to Stony Crick after all. Maybe even by summer, Jeremy thought.

At about this time, Fenn got married. After that he didn't stop by the way he used to, but when he'd been married a few weeks, he came over and asked them all to dinner in his new apartment. They'd never laid eyes on his wife—Shirley, her name was. She was a girl who worked in the factory, and she'd always lived in Chicago.

Fenn had moved into a building about four blocks away. He was waiting for them at the entrance downstairs because he was afraid they wouldn't know how to use the elevator.

"I could've done it," Johnson said ungratefully.

"You know about as much about an elevator as a hog knows about Sunday. You've never even been in one," Ethan told him.

Johnson shoved Ethan, and he almost knocked over a big jar full of sand to put cigarette ashes in. Ma grabbed Johnson by the collar. "Comin' to a fine place like this and actin' like savages," she jawed at them.

Jeremy didn't like being squinched up in the elevator. Ethan was breathing down his neck, and Pa's elbow was in his ear. They had a terrible time getting Homer D. in. He dug his heels intó the floor, and Pa had to carry him in stiff as a board. It seemed like they'd never get up to the fifth floor, where Fenn lived. Ethan and Johnson liked it though. They were all for going down again and coming up by themselves, but Ma put a stop to that.

When Shirley opened the door, Caroline said, "Oh, she's pretty."

"Pretty," Homer D. said.

And Shirley was. She had blond curls piled up high on top of her head, and she wore beautiful, long silver earrings and a red dress without any sleeves even if it was almost winter.

If Caroline was pleased with Shirley, she was speechless over the apartment. They'd none of them ever seen anything like it before. The bright blue rug on the floor was so thick they could hardly pull their feet out of it. It was broad daylight outside, but in here they had the lights on because the windows were smothered with heavy green-and-purple-flowered curtains. Jeremy had never seen a room so full of things. There was a big green sofa piled high with tiny blue, yellow, and pink pillows and there were two big green chairs and half a dozen little tables. The tables were covered with little scarves and doilies, and the scarves and doilies were covered with ash trays and vases and little china figures. All the chairs faced one wall, which was taken up by the biggest television set Jeremy had ever seen. It was all covered with doilies and ash trays and vases and little figures, too.

Caroline stayed close to Shirley, but Ethan and Johnson ran ahead into the kitchen. Now they hollered for Jeremy to come out and see it. He had to squeeze past the biggest icebox in the world to get in. It was so big it stuck out past the doorway and covered almost half of one wall. Shirley came out and showed them how the stove worked. Things turned on and off by themselves and bells rang and lights flashed on. That stove could probably take off and fly anyplace all by itself.

After supper, Fenn said, "I've saved the best for the last." He walked over and turned on the big television set, and the pictures were in color.

"Would you look at that?" Pa said. "They keep sayin' on TV that the pictures are in livin' color, but I never saw one before that was."

"I always thought they was lyin'," Johnson said.

"We haven't seen TV since we came," Caroline said. "The Eustises had one at home."

Nobody could get a word in edgewise all the way home. Caroline kept jabbering about the TV set and the blue taffeta bedspread on the bed and the fluffy white rug by the bathtub.

Ma snorted at that. "If she had five young'uns, she

wouldn't've bought a white rug. When it comes right down to it, Fenn's shoes are probably none too clean, either. And speakin' of Fenn, where'd he scrape up the money to pay for those trappin's?"

"Trappin's, Ma? Wasn't it beautiful?" Caroline asked, but Ma didn't answer.

Pa said, "Fenn didn't pay for nothing yet. He just pays for it all a week at a time, a few dollars here and a few dollars there."

"And all the stuff's wore out before it's ever paid for," Ma said. "I'm thankful we don't have no call to live like that."

"Oh, I don't know," Pa said. "I don't know's I'd want to go in as deep as Fenn, but it don't seem wrong to enjoy somethin' like say a TV set while you're savin' up for it."

"If you can't pay for it, you got no business havin' it," Ma said, so it looked like they wouldn't have a TV set for a while.

But they did. On Pa's next day off somebody knocked at the door and Ethan opened it. A strange man said, "We got your TV set."

Ethan said, "Wow!" and opened the door wider.

"We didn't ask for any TV set," Ma said.

Pa got up with a sheepish look on his face. "Well, I was goin' to wait till Christmas," he said, "but they was havin' such a special price, a feller couldn't hardly afford not to buy one now."

"Now!" Homer D. said. "Now!" He clapped his hands.

Ma opened her mouth, but she looked at the man at the door and didn't say a word. She wouldn't fault Pa before a stranger. She went into the bedroom and shut the door.

The men who brought the TV set turned it on before they left, and everybody watched it all the rest of the day.

They even watched while they ate their supper, and they watched past bedtime. Ma kept herself busy all the time, but Jeremy noticed that she watched once in a while out of the corner of her eye.

There were mountains in one of the stories, and it was all so real that Jeremy could almost smell the pine needles in the sun. If he couldn't have the real thing for a while, this was better than nothing.

He couldn't get to sleep right away that night and he heard Pa and Ma talking in the bedroom. Lots of times he could hear them talking after he went to bed, but he'd never heard them talk so loud before.

"Now own up you liked it," Pa coaxed. "Own up it was a good idea."

But Ma was stubborn. "Anything that keeps us one day longer away from Stony Crick's not a good idea."

"I'm makin' good money."

"But it goes out as fast as it comes in. We don't want to live the rest of our lives here, do we?"

Jeremy didn't hear Pa's answer. That worried him some. Surely Pa wasn't getting to like it here. How could anybody?

It didn't take long for Jeremy to get almighty tired of that TV. It was on all day long, from getting up till past bedtime. Sometimes Pa'd get so interested in a story he'd keep it on long after the boys had gone to bed.

Homer D. didn't take to TV, either. The first few days he was hunched up in front of it most of the time, but after that, whenever it was on, he sat in a corner with his face turned to the wall. Ethan and Johnson laughed at him, but Jeremy knew just how he felt. He was sure Homer D. understood a lot more than anybody gave him credit for, and he believed Pa was wrong about Homer D. learning his letters. If things ever quieted down, he'd have to help Homer D. with them again.

Things at school weren't getting any better. You'd think he'd tried to do Nick a hurt instead of the other way around. Nick went out of his way to be mean every time he had a chance. Once he grabbed Jeremy's homework paper and crumpled it up before Jeremy had time to hand it in. There wasn't time to copy it over. He tried to straighten it out, but Mrs. McNutt gave him a zero for having a messy paper. It didn't take much to get a zero from Mrs. McNutt. Jeremy'd gone right on turning down the boys on the playground when they got around to choosing him near the end, and now they didn't bother to choose him at all. And it seemed he couldn't open his mouth without being straightened out by Mrs. McNutt or laughed at by somebody else. Well, he'd heard Pa say you could stand anything for a year, and they'd be home before that. Ma was still managing to put something by every week since Pa'd got his job at the garage.

If it wasn't for Mr. Sherman, things would be even worse. He'd helped Jeremy get a library card, and Jeremy could bring home four books every week. After Homer D. tore a page out of one, Jeremy took to keeping them in Mr. Sherman's apartment and reading down there. He really wasn't afraid of Baron any more, but he still felt a little more comfortable if the dog wasn't too close. He just never could quite get used to Baron sitting there, staring at him with his tongue lolling out like he was licking his chops.

Sometimes he and Mr. Sherman talked about all kinds of things, and sometimes they just sat there and read without saying a word.

It seemed like Mr. Sherman was the only one he did talk

to any more. Ethan and Johnson and Caroline were always out playing someplace, and you couldn't really talk to Homer D. Ma stayed in her room a lot with the door shut, and Pa never got home till time to eat. All through supper and till bedtime the TV blatted on and on.

# 10

## Arthur

One morning just before Thanksgiving, Mrs. McNutt was writing on the blackboard. She had just written, "The breaking waves dashed high," when there was a sort of scratching at the door. Mrs. McNutt went on writing, and in a minute there was another noise, so faint it was like something brushing against the door.

"Someone's at the door, Mrs. McNutt," Darlene Baker said. Since Mrs. McNutt had her back to them, she couldn't fault Darlene for not raising her hand. Slowly the teacher turned around and wiped the chalk dust from her hands with a piece of tissue. Then she stalked over to the door and flung it open.

A small boy with a shock of mousey blond hair hanging down to his eyebrows stumbled into the room. Mrs. McNutt reached out for the big white card he held, but instead he stretched out his bony right hand and touched her soft white one. She drew it back as if she'd been snake-bit. Everyone laughed fit to kill. Joe pounded his desk and drummed his heels on the floor. Darlene Baker turned around and grinned at Jeremy, the first time she'd so much as looked at him since the day he'd worn the dirty shirt and she'd held her nose. Surprised, he grinned back and laughed out loud like the rest of them.

Then he looked at the boy and felt ashamed. How could he have forgotten so fast how it felt to be the one standing there with his hand stuck out and a foolish look on his face like something the cat dragged in and forgot to kill?

Mrs. McNutt clapped her hands once. "You will come to order immediately," she snapped. She looked at the white card in her hand. "Arthur May, from Kentucky," she said with the mean smile that Jeremy hated. She said Kentucky like it was a contagious disease.

"Well, Arthur May, you'll have to sit on this chair by my desk until the custodian can bring in another desk for you."

"Arthur May," Harry snickered in back of him. "That's real pretty." He clapped Jeremy on the back. Yesterday Jeremy would have given just about anything to be in on a joke, but now he didn't turn around.

He tried hard not to look at Arthur May, but he couldn't help it. Arthur looked down as if there was something that interested him on the floor, but his face was fiery red and his hands were clenched at his side.

Mrs. McNutt sent Nick to tell Mr. Jenks they needed another desk, and in the middle of math, Mr. Jenks came puffing in with it. "It's kind of beat up," he apologized, and it was. There was a slat missing out of the seat back, and the whole back end of the desk part was gone and you could see all the way through it.

"It's quite all right," Mrs. McNutt said carelessly, as if anything was good enough for Arthur May. She went to the squatty bookcase under the window and took out half a dozen books and laid them on Arthur's desk. Arthur nervously stuffed them inside, and they promptly slid through the open back to the floor. Even Jeremy couldn't help laughing this time—until he caught sight of Arthur's face as he crawled around on the floor after the books.

While Arthur was still down there, the bell rang for lunch, and he jumped and hit his head on the underneath side of his desk.

Jeremy walked over, picked up the last book and stuffed it carefully in the front part of the desk.

"C'mon, Arthur," he said. "I'll show you where the cafeteria is." It was nice to have somebody to walk with.

He showed Arthur where to get his fork and spoon, and they shoved their trays down the line.

The cross-eyed, red-headed serving lady was working today. "Woodchuck or Sloppy Joe?" she asked, her spoon poised impatiently over the steam table.

Arthur's face lighted up. "Woodchuck," he said happily before Jeremy could stop him. The serving lady dipped her spoon into a kettle and poured a brownish-red mixture over a slice of bread on a blue plastic plate.

"That's not woodchuck," Arthur said.

"I tried to tell you," Jeremy said. "It's what they call woodchuck here; I never did find out why."

"I'm not hungry anyway," Arthur told him.

When they sat down, Joe and Nick were already seated across from them at the table. "Guess what," Joe called to someone at the end of the table. "We got a boy named May in our room. Ain't he pretty?"

"Leave him alone," Jeremy surprised himself by saying. Arthur just stared at his plate without picking up his fork.

"Don't tell me who to leave alone, hillbilly," Joe said.

Jeremy laid down his fork. All of a sudden he wasn't hungry, either. He didn't have any friends, but at least they hadn't name-called him for quite a while. Now the tormenting was going to start again, all on account of Arthur.

But maybe it was better to have one friend and be tormented for it than not to have any friends at all. Jeremy could hardly wait for school to be over so he could find out more about Arthur.

It really felt good having somebody to walk down the street with, even if Nick and Joe were hooting, "Leatherhead and Mayflower; they stink worse every hour," behind them.

Arthur was really wound up. "Why'd they want to call that stuff woodchuck? It's not fair to call something woodchuck and have it not be woodchuck. I bet they never even saw one."

They both rounded the corner at the same place, and it turned out that Arthur only lived about a block away from Jeremy.

A little way from home Jeremy saw Mr. Sherman and Baron walking ahead of them.

"C'mon," Jeremy said to Arthur, who was still going on about woodchucks, "I'll make you acquainted with Mr. Sherman. Hi, Mr. Sherman!"

Just as Mr. Sherman turned around to answer, Nick and Joe popped out from around the corner and hollered, "Hillbillies!"

"You must have a friend with you," Mr. Sherman said when they caught up with him. "I suppose you've noticed by now that the name 'hillbilly' gets handed down like an outgrown pair of shoes."

"I do have a friend with me." Jeremy's tongue lingered

pleasantly over the word *friend.* "This is Arthur May, but what did you mean about the shoes?"

"You must know that half the people in your room have come from the hills some time or other. The last person in has to be the goat. When the next person comes along, the one before gets out from under by passing the teasing on to him."

"You mean Nick and Joe come from the hills?"

"Might be. A lot of them try to cover it up after a while." Mr. Sherman knew a lot about all kinds of things.

"What for? I'll bet there's more good men come from Kentucky than Chicago any day in the week."

"I wouldn't argue with you about that," Mr. Sherman laughed.

The next morning when he woke up Jeremy couldn't think why he felt so good, but he soon remembered. He had a friend—a friend to eat lunch with and walk home with and go to the library with.

The boys had just started down the walk when Jeremy saw Arthur at the corner. "My friend's waiting for me," he said importantly to Ethan and Johnson. It was the first time anybody had ever waited for him in Chicago.

"Hi," Arthur called. "Did you get your homework done? I didn't. I never had any like that before, and my dad said he never did, either."

Jeremy opened his mouth to at least say "Hi," but Arthur never stopped long enough for him to get a word in edgewise.

"Does that Mr. Sherman take his dog to school with him every day? Doesn't he ever bark?"

Jeremy would've liked to tell Arthur about Baron, but Arthur never stopped talking to listen. Now he was talking about how bad the water was in Chicago. Jeremy didn't like the taste of the water, either, but listening to Arthur carry on about it made him feel as if he ought to say something good about it if he ever got a chance.

It sure was nice having a friend to walk with, though. And it was nice having a partner at lunch, too. Today they had Rice Surprise.

"Couldn't be any more of a surprise than that woodchuck," Arthur said, looking at the steaming mound on his plate.

"I don't know," Jeremy said. "You never can tell what they'll put in a surprise." He poked around in the rice until he found five small bites of ham, which he pushed to one side of his plate. "I like to know ahead of time what I'm eating," he said cautiously.

"Me, too. Last night we had hot dogs for dinner. We never had hot dogs in Kentucky, but Ma says we'll have them a lot up here. She cooks them good."

Somehow or other Arthur managed to talk and eat at the same time, so his plate was empty by the time the bell rang.

He stuck close to Jeremy all the way upstairs, talking about hot dogs all the way.

"Leatherhead and Mayflower; they stink worse every hour," Nick whispered in back of them, looking as if butter wouldn't melt in his mouth. It had started all over again, the teasing and meanness he thought Nick and the others had got tired of.

The next day was Saturday, and he had some books to take back to the library. When he first met Arthur he'd thought it would be nice to have someone to walk to the library with, but something told him that Arthur wouldn't like the library, so he didn't ask him to go. It didn't matter, though, because Jeremy'd barely got out on the sidewalk when he caught sight of him.

"Hey," Arthur called out, "what are we gonna do today?"

"Before we do anything, I have to take these books back to the library."

"Okay. Where is it?" Arthur asked, running to catch up with him.

He chattered all the way to the library, but Jeremy only halfway listened. At least Arthur would have to be quiet when they got there.

Jeremy always liked to stand inside the doorway of the little, dimly lit room, just breathing in the dusty, bookish smell for a minute. Now Arthur bumped into him from the back.

"Golly," he said, without even lowering his voice, "lookit all those books. I never saw so many. Who's going to read them all?"

Jeremy hoped Miss Robbins would be there today. He really liked her the best because she always called him by name and tried to help him find the books he'd like. She had dark skin and hair that must have been frizzed out a foot all the way around her head. He imagined Ma would say it looked outlandish, but he thought it looked nice on Miss Robbins.

She wasn't at the desk today, though. Instead the sour-faced lady, with her hair stretched to a tight bun in back of her ears, sat there. She always looked as if she hoped no one would come in to mess up her books.

She frowned at Arthur now. "This is a library," she whispered exaggeratedly.

"We know. My friend has some books to bring back," Arthur told her in a friendly voice.

The librarian's face was red. "You should know," she said, forgetting to whisper, "that we do not talk out loud in a library."

"Oh, don't we?" Arthur looked surprised.

Jeremy quickly laid his books on the desk and tiptoed to the farthest corner, hoping that Arthur wouldn't follow. But that was too good to be true. He could hear the slip-slop of Arthur's untied sneakers behind him. Jeremy pulled out the first book he could find and buried his nose in it.

"Is that a good one? Can you take any one you want to? Maybe I'll take one, too." Arthur had a penetrating whisper.

The librarian looked at them, but she didn't say anything. Arthur was whispering all right, even if he did sound like a bullfrog with the croup.

Jeremy grabbed four books off the shelf without even looking to see what they were—just to get out of the library. One of them turned out to be *Prudence of the Parsonage.* No wonder the librarian had given him a funny look. He'd certainly have to put it someplace where Ethan and Johnson wouldn't see it. The other three didn't look so bad; he could hardly wait to get home and start reading. But Arthur followed him up the stairs and into the house, and Ma was so pleased to see Jeremy with a friend that she invited him to stay for lunch, in spite of Jeremy standing in back of Arthur and shaking his head.

Arthur stayed all afternoon and probably would have stayed for supper if Jeremy hadn't thought to get him out in the yard before Ma could ask him.

By the middle of the week, Jeremy couldn't remember why he'd thought he wanted a friend. He hadn't known when he was well off. Arthur was waiting for him every morning to walk to school and every afternoon to walk home again. And now he'd probably go to the library with him every Saturday. Jeremy thought about all the Saturdays when he'd spent all morning at the library, reading from one book after another to see whether he wanted to take them home or not. He would never have ended up with *Prudence of the Parsonage* before Arthur came. The quiet afternoons of reading at Mr. Sherman's apartment were gone, too.

Thursday Arthur didn't show up at school, and Jeremy went to Mr. Sherman's apartment as soon as he got home. It might help to talk things over with him.

"Where's your friend Arthur?" Mr. Sherman asked.

"He wasn't at school today," Jeremy answered. He tried not to say anything more, but the first thing he knew the words were tumbling out. "I thought Arthur would be a friend, but he isn't. A friend likes what you like, and he listens to what you want to talk about sometimes. I wish I'd never tried to help Arthur."

When Mr. Sherman heard about how it all started, he smiled. "Well, Jeremy," he said, "there was an Oriental custom that if you saved a person's life, you were responsible for that person as long as he lived."

Jeremy thought about Arthur jabbering along at his elbow for the rest of his life. He wondered if he could stand it till they left for Stony Crick.

# 11

## God Rest Ye Merry

Ma always said, "Be careful what you wish for; it might come true," and she was right. One morning after Arthur had only been there about two weeks, he had a long face when he met Jeremy to walk to school.

"I'm goin' away," he said. "My uncle in Detroit's found a job for Pa, and we're movin' next week."

For a few days after Arthur left, Jeremy was happy. He read more in two days than he'd read in the whole time since Arthur had come. He worked with Homer D. on his ABC's and Homer D. almost seemed to like it. Jeremy spent all the time he wanted to at the library. But by the following week, he began to have an empty feeling. After Arthur left, they'd quit teasing him. Maybe Nick and Joe couldn't find any good rhymes for Leatherhead. Anyway they'd gone back to leaving him strictly alone. At least Arthur had really liked him. Maybe it was better to have a friend you didn't like than not to have any at all.

The only good thing about school now was Miss Collins, the music teacher who came on Thursdays. Today she was making all the boys try out for a part in the Christmas program.

"God rest ye merry, Gentlemen; let nothing you dismay." Jeremy's voice was clear and steady even though this was the first time he'd sung alone since they'd left Stony Crick. Most of the boys were trying to scrunch down behind their desks, but Jeremy didn't mind being called. Singing was one thing he knew he could do.

"Very good," Miss Collins said. She sounded surprised. "Why haven't I heard you sing out like that before?"

"You didn't ask me before," Jeremy answered.

Ben was next. If it wasn't for the words, you'd never have guessed what he was singing. He didn't even wait for Miss Collins to tell him to sit down.

And no one else could sing worth beans till Nick got up. He swaggered up to the front and began to sing almost before Miss Collins could get to the piano. He was good, too. Jeremy had to admit if there was one thing Nick could do, it was sing. He'd surely be the one chosen.

"Nick's always best," he heard Darlene whispering in back of him.

Miss Collins was looking down at the keyboard, tapping a pencil against her teeth. In a minute she looked up, her blue eyes sparkling.

"It was hard to make a decision this year," she said, "but I think I will have to choose Jeremy Weatherhead."

Jeremy couldn't believe his ears. It was the first time he'd been chosen to do anything first since he came here. He felt good, like he belonged. But when he looked over at the other side of the room, he could see that Nick's face was as red as fire. If it wasn't Nick, Jeremy would have thought he was about to cry.

Mrs. McNutt always left the room when Miss Collins was there. When she came back, Darlene said, "Guess

*90*

what, Mrs. McNutt. Nick isn't going to sing the solo this year; Jeremy is."

"What if there's a fire drill?" Nick muttered loud enough so everybody could hear. They all laughed. Even Mrs. McNutt smiled her tight little smile. The belonging feeling was gone. He was Jeremy—Leatherhead again.

Even so, he could hardly wait to tell Ethan and Johnson on the way home.

"You mean you're going to sing in front of everybody all by yourself? Golly, I wouldn't want to do that," Johnson said.

"Nobody'd want you to. You can't sing as good as a hoot owl," Ethan jeered.

Johnson took out after Ethan, and that was the end of talk about the Christmas program as far as they were concerned.

Mr. Sherman came along before Jeremy got home. Jeremy told him the news.

"You must have sung pretty well; Miss Collins is hard to please," Mr. Sherman said.

Jeremy could hardly wait to tell Ma, but when he burst into the apartment, she wasn't there. By the time she got back with the groceries, she was in a hurry to fix supper. Caroline and Homer D. had a cartoon show blasting full-tilt on the television.

He managed to tell his news after Pa got home, when they all sat down to supper. Pa and Ma were so proud to hear all about it that Pa turned off the TV set and didn't turn it on again till after they were through eating.

While Ma washed the dishes, Jeremy wiped them. Just one thing worried him. He stood up close so they could talk over the noise of "Gilligan's Island."

"Ma," he said, "we wouldn't be going before then, would we?"

"Going where before when?" Ma asked.

"Going back to Stony Crick before Christmas."

"It don't seem likely," Ma said dryly. "We'll be lucky if we get there by summertime."

Jeremy never thought he'd be glad of anything that kept him in Chicago another day, but he couldn't help wanting to stay till after the program.

It was going to be a long time till next Thursday when Miss Collins came again, but just having something to look forward to made school seem a little better.

All day Wednesday he kept wondering how it would be. Would Miss Collins call him up to stand beside the piano and sing, or would he just stand by his own desk? Anyhow everybody would have to be quiet and listen to him, and maybe for once they wouldn't find anything to laugh about.

Jeremy was so wrapped up in his own thoughts he forgot to listen to Mrs. McNutt.

". . . I'll leave the room, and I'll give you five minutes to return it to my desk. If it isn't there, you're all in trouble." He wished he'd heard what Mrs. McNutt was talking about.

After the door closed behind Mrs. McNutt, everyone was quiet. Then there was a babble.

"C'mon, you rat, whoever you are, put it back," Jerry said. "When old lady McNutt says we'll all be in trouble, she means it."

Jeremy couldn't stand it any longer. "Put what back?" he asked Darlene.

"Her paperweight, Leatherhead. Don't you ever listen?"

Jeremy had never seen anything like Mrs. McNutt's paperweight. A tiny deer stood among miniature ever-greens in a little glass globe. When the paperweight was shaken, snowflakes swirled around through the trees like a real storm was coming up. He wondered who could have taken it. If he was ever going to steal anything, it certainly wouldn't be from Mrs. McNutt.

He didn't know five minutes could be so long. At first there were giggles and jokes, but the closer the five minutes came to being over, the quieter the room grew. No one moved a muscle when Mrs. McNutt opened the door and walked over to her desk. She stared at the empty space where the paperweight had been, and then looked at the class.

"Raise the lids on your desks and fold your hands in your laps." Jeremy felt sorry for whoever had taken the paperweight. Mrs. McNutt's words sounded cold and hard, like stones being dropped into a well one at a time.

Usually desk lids were opened with thumps and thuds, but this time there wasn't a sound. Mrs. McNutt stood watching until every desk was opened, and then she started slowly up the aisle by the window, stopping a long minute to peer into each desk.

Jeremy was in the second row beyond the window, and he could feel goose bumps coming out on his arms when he heard Mrs. McNutt at the desk behind his, even though he knew he hadn't done anything.

Then she was standing beside his desk. When she leaned over, he could see the straight part in her hair, like she'd made it with a ruler. And then she was standing up, and the paperweight was in her hand.

"All right, Jeremy. Stand up and come with me. The rest of you get out your spelling books and study page forty-nine. Darlene, you sit at my desk and take the name of anyone who is disorderly."

Jeremy hardly knew what he was doing as he followed Mrs. McNutt to the door. How could the paperweight have gotten into his desk?

Mrs. McNutt marched him down the hall toward the office of the principal, Mr. Harper, her fingers digging into his shoulders. Once he looked up at her, wanting to say he didn't know how the paperweight got there, but he couldn't make the words come out.

Gertie, who'd taken him to his room on the first day of school, was sitting at the desk in the room outside Mr. Harper's private office.

"Is Mr. Harper busy?" Mrs. McNutt's fingers dug deeper into Jeremy's shoulder.

"Mr. Sherman's with him now," Gertie said, looking at Jeremy curiously.

Mrs. McNutt sat down on a little bench and pulled Jeremy down beside her. At least she wasn't holding his shoulder any more, but he didn't like sitting so close to her. He held himself stiffly, trying not to touch her. Now it was too late to say he hadn't taken the paperweight; he didn't want to talk about it in front of Gertie. Besides, he didn't want to be talking when Mr. Sherman came out. If he kept quiet, Mr. Sherman would never know he was in the office.

It seemed as if he and Mrs. McNutt had been sitting there together on that little bench forever, waiting for Mr. Harper's door to open. His thoughts were chasing around in his head without any more sense than a squirrel running up and down a tree trunk. If the paperweight was in his desk, someone had put it there, and who would do a thing like that? He didn't know anyone that mean. Or did he? All of a sudden he could see the hate shining out of Nick's black eyes when Miss Collins said, "I will have to choose Jeremy Weatherhead."

The door opened, and Mr. Sherman and Baron came out. It was a good thing Baron wasn't like most dogs. He never even looked toward Jeremy; Mr. Sherman wouldn't know there was anyone he knew in the room.

Mrs. McNutt didn't wait for Gertie to tell them to go in. She stood up and pushed Jeremy ahead of her through the open door. He was surprised to see a tall, red-headed young man standing in back of the desk. He'd never really seen Mr. Harper, but from the talk he'd heard, he thought he'd be an old man with heavy black eyebrows and a scowl. And he'd thought the office would be dark, with bars over the windows and different-sized whips hanging all over the walls. He hadn't expected this sunny room with the light-green curtains and the picture of a pretty young woman and a little boy on a bookcase under the window.

He almost forgot why he was there until he heard Mrs. McNutt's voice behind him.

"This is Jeremy Weatherhead," she said.

"Oh, the newcomer who reorganized the fire drill," Mr. Harper said. He looked as if he were trying not to smile.

Mrs. McNutt didn't have any trouble not smiling. "What he did at the fire drill may have been excusable, though if he'd been listening, he wouldn't have done it. But what he did today was not excusable under any circumstances. Even a mountain child should be expected to know that stealing is wrong."

"I didn't steal anything," Jeremy said. "I wouldn't."

"Don't interrupt. When I saw that my paperweight was missing, I gave the thief every opportunity to put it back, but I had to search the desks to find it." She was still holding the paperweight in her hand.

Jeremy didn't know how he could ever have thought it was pretty.

"Why did you take the paperweight, Jeremy?" Mr. Harper's eyes seemed to look right through him.

"I didn't take it," Jeremy said. Mr. Harper would surely believe him if anybody would.

"Then do you have any idea how it got in your desk?"

Jeremy hesitated. He couldn't give Nick a bad name when he didn't know for sure what happened. "No, sir," he mumbled, "I don't know."

"Of course he knows," Mrs. McNutt said. "There's only one way for it to have gotten there. I've seen the way he looked at that paperweight every time he came close to the desk; he wanted it and he took it. It's as simple as that."

"Stealing is a serious thing," Mr. Harper said.

As if anybody had to tell him stealing was wrong. Why, he'd been taught not only not to steal, but not to even want anything that belonged to anybody else. He hadn't wanted Mrs. McNutt's paperweight; why would he when it was there for the looking? Thinking about that now, he missed part of what was being said, as usual.

". . . no recess for a month," Mrs. McNutt was saying. At least that wouldn't bother him any. "Also, Miss Collins chose Jeremy for a solo part in the Christmas program, and it would not be a good example for the children to see their room represented by a thief."

A thief? She couldn't be talking about him. Pa and Ma would die of shame if they ever heard such a thing.

Mr. Harper looked almost as if he was afraid of Mrs. McNutt, too. Jeremy thought maybe if he could just be alone with Mr. Harper, he could make the principal believe he really didn't know what happened. But he wasn't going to have that chance. Mrs. McNutt was pushing him back out of the door ahead of her. He didn't even look at Gertie as they went through the other room to the hall.

Ever since last week he'd been looking forward to Thursday, and now he knew it was going to be the worst day he'd had at school yet.

When Miss Collins came, she only looked at him briefly, but he could see the puzzlement in her eyes. Would she say anything about why he wasn't going to sing? He didn't think Nick even knew that yet.

But she didn't shame Jeremy in front of the class. When it came time to sing "God Rest Ye Merry, Gentlemen," she just called Nick up and told him to try it, like she'd never even had them try out the week before. And she smiled at Jeremy the same as at everyone else.

Now that that part was over with, he could start thinking about how he'd tell his folks he wasn't going to sing by himself. Maybe they'd forgotten about it anyway. Nobody'd brought it up again since he first told them about it.

But that night at supper, during a TV commercial, Pa said, "I saw Fenn today and invited him and Shirley to the Christmas doin's at the school. I knew they'd be proud to hear Jeremy sing."

Jeremy almost choked on a big piece of potato and had to take a big swig of milk to make it go down. "I don't know if we can bring anybody else or not," he said.

"Yes, we can," Ethan said. "Our teacher said all our friends and relatives could come."

"That's a good thing," Pa said. "It'd be right unmannerly to uninvite Fenn and Shirley after I'd already asked 'em to come."

"Oh, look!" Caroline said. "That's Burpy Betty! That's the doll I been tellin' you about, Ma. Look at her; she drinks and wets and burps and everything."

Maybe Caroline was a rattlebrain, but she sure came in handy for changing the subject.

Every morning he thought he'd tell Ma that day, and every night he couldn't. Thursdays were the worst of all. It was hard to have Nick stand up next to Miss Collins and sing the song he should have been singing. And Nick had a way of saying things like, "If you can't sing good, sing loud, Leatherhead. I'll need a loud chorus to back me up."

One night shortly before the program, Pa said, "Harriet, take this boy out and get him a new pair of pants. We don't want him to get up to sing lookin' like he's wearin' Johnson's clothes."

"What's wrong with my clothes?" Johnson asked.

"Nothin', on you, but they'd fit Jeremy a mite too soon."

"Well, reckon I could use this week's Stony Crick money," Ma said slowly. "Jeremy needs a new pair anyhow, and Johnson can take the old ones."

"Don't use the goin'-back-home money, Ma. My pants are all right," Jeremy told her. But when he got home from school the next day, Ma was waiting to take him to the store.

All the way to the store he tried to tell Ma he wouldn't be singing alone, but he just couldn't, not after she said, "We're right proud, Jeremy, that you got picked for this so soon after we come." Ma never was much of a hand to brag on them. He almost wished he'd get hit by a truck. Ma picked out a pair of dark-blue pants so long he'd have to wear them forever, and he knew he'd hate them the rest of his life.

He'd never known the days to go so fast. Two nights before the program, Fenn came over and said, "I'm right sorry, but I'm set on takin' Shirley to meet the folks at home before Christmas, and it looks like we can't make it to the doin's at school."

Well, at least Jeremy wouldn't be shamed in front of Fenn and Shirley. Now if he could only think of some way to keep the rest of them at home. But with four kids in the program and Ma spending her Stony Crick money for a new pair of pants, it would take a miracle, and he'd never heard of God making any miracles in Chicago.

The next morning when Jeremy woke up, Homer D. was standing by the window. "Look," he said, grinning. "Look!"

Jeremy'd never seen such a sight. The whole outside was white. You couldn't tell what was yard and what was alley. Everything looked strange and different. Even the old cars in the yard looked mysterious under their covering of snow, like giant mushrooms that had shot up overnight. And more snow was coming down so fast you could hardly see out of the window.

Pa bundled up and started out for work, but he came back in a few minutes. "Nothin' runnin'," he said, "and it's unpossible to walk. There won't be no work today, nor no school, either."

"It's got to quit before tomorrow," Caroline wailed. "Tomorrow's the Christmas program."

But it didn't quit all that day nor that night, either. By morning they knew there couldn't possibly be any school or any Christmas program.

Ma tried to comfort Jeremy. "It's not as if you hadn't been chose," she said. "That's the important thing. You'll have another chance."

"It's all right, Ma." Ma couldn't know how right it was.

If he was lucky, they'd be back in Stony Crick before he ever had another such chance.

# 12

## Maybe Never

"Isn't it beautiful? I wish we'd never take it down."
Caroline was jumping up and down in front of the silver
tree that was their Christmas present from Fenn and
Shirley. Jeremy remembered how disappointed he'd been
when they brought it over.

"It won't shed on the floor nor nothing, and it'll last
forever," Shirley had said proudly. "We thought the kids
would like it."

Like it? How could anybody like a Christmas tree that
wasn't green and didn't smell like a tree? But the others
didn't seem to mind.

He'd heard Pa and Ma talking about it after they'd gone
to bed.

"It'd be unmannerly and wasteful not to use the ugly
thing now they've brought it, but why did they? For one
thing, we never toted gifts all over, and now we'll have to
go out and buy something for them."

"Harriet Weatherhead, I'm 'shamed to hear you talk so

miserly. I guess we can afford to get presents for our kinfolk. And I don't know why you call that tree so ugly."

"If you don't know that, then there's no use talkin' to you."

But Jeremy never heard Ma fault the tree again. The last day before school was out, they all brought home the decorations they'd made out of paper—green and red chains and stars and angels and lopsided lanterns. But no matter what they put on it, that tree didn't look any better. To Jeremy it always looked like it was too proud to wear their homemade decorations and was trying to throw them off.


On Christmas morning, they all stood around the tree and waited for Pa and Ma to come out of their room. When they did come out, Pa was shoving a box so big he couldn't lift it, and Ma was wheeling out a doll buggy with a doll in it.

"Burpy Betty! Burpy Betty!" Caroline squealed. "I knew I'd get her. I knew it!"

"Who's the big box for?" Ethan asked.

"It's for all you boys. Go ahead and open it." Pa was beaming at them.

All three of them began to dig into the box. Inside were more little boxes wrapped in brown paper. Johnson got the first one unwrapped.

"Oh, Pa!" he said. "You got us a Zoomer, a real Zoomer."

There'd be a lot of kids with real Zoomers if the TV people had their way, Jeremy thought. It seemed like for weeks you could hardly turn on the TV without hearing how nobody could get along without at least one slot-car home raceway.

He'd thought he never wanted to hear about a Zoomer again, but just the same he was excited now as they began to unwrap the pieces of track. Ethan and Johnson got in two or three fights before they were through, but Pa got right down on the floor and helped put the track together. It really was something the way those little cars chased each other around it.

Ma watched them, sitting bolt upright on the big new sofa. Pa'd had it brought home yesterday for a surprise present for Ma. Jeremy could tell from her face that it wasn't a surprise that made Ma happy, but Pa'd said there was no reason she shouldn't have things just as nice as Shirley's. Even Pa'd had to admit it looked bigger up here than it had in the store. They'd tried it every place. The TV was on one wall. Another wall had the door to Pa's and Ma's room. If they put it along the third wall, they'd have to climb over it every time they went outside. And the window was in the fourth wall. They ended up with the sofa in the middle of the room, facing the TV set with its back to the stove and icebox. Ma had to squeeze past it every time she went from the stove to the table. They moved the table in back of the sofa, and when they sat down to eat, Caroline almost had her head in the oven.

"I still can't believe we've really got our own Zoomer," Johnson kept saying.

"Zoomer." Homer D. was sitting cross-legged on the floor as far away from the Christmas tree and the Zoomer as he could get.

"Land sakes," Ma said, "how could we of forgot?" She went back to the clothes closet and brought out a fuzzy horse almost as big as Homer D.

Caroline dropped her doll. "Oh, look, Homer D.," she said. "You could ride him. He even has a saddle."

Homer D. wouldn't touch that horse. Pa and Ma tried not to act put out because Homer D. didn't take to his present, but Jeremy knew they were disappointed. There was no figuring Homer D. out. He just was the way he was.

Jeremy kept wondering when he should bring his presents out. He knew it wouldn't be any use right now. He'd been proud of the things he'd bought with the money he earned doing errands for Mr. Sherman, but they didn't hold a candle to the Zoomer.

Ma finally got them all to the table for breakfast. While she was dishing up the grits, Jeremy handed around the packages Mr. Sherman had helped him wrap—the bunched-up ones for Johnson and Ethan and Caroline, the square one for Homer D., and the big, flat one for Ma and Pa.

Ethan had his unwrapped first. He looked at the big pottery pig. "What's it for?" he asked.

"To save money for Stony Crick," Jeremy told him.

"Oh. Well, it sure is nice." Ethan started in on his grits.

Johnson and Caroline didn't have much to say about their banks, either. Caroline put hers down beside her bowl and said, "I wish we'd got to make presents the way we always did before."

Jeremy thought about the things they used to make for each other at Christmas. Those presents weren't any great shakes, but it didn't take as much to make a present in Stony Crick. It seemed like in Chicago nobody set any store by anything unless it was something boughten.

Ma helped Homer D. to open his blocks, and Jeremy tried to show him how to build something, but he wouldn't touch the blocks any more than he had the horse.

Jeremy could hardly wait for Ma and Pa to open their

present. When he'd first seen that picture in the dime store, he'd stood right in the aisle and looked at it till somebody ran into him. It looked exactly like the sun setting behind Blue Mountain. It cost a heap—a dollar and twenty-nine cents—but of course you'd expect to pay a lot for a picture like that.

Ma unwrapped it, and for a little spell she and Pa didn't say a word. Then Pa said, "That shore is purty, Jeremy."

Ma said, "If that don't look for all the world like the sun goin' down behind Blue Mountain," and there were tears in her eyes. Jeremy didn't want Ma to cry, but he was proud she felt the same way he did about that picture.

"Maybe it won't be too long till we'll be seein' Blue Mountain," Jeremy said.

"Might be," Ma said. But Pa didn't say anything.

After breakfast, Caroline looked out of the window and saw the Buckhorn girls in the yard, tramping around in the dirty snow in new white boots and scooping up melting snow with soggy, white fur mittens.

Ma shook her head. "Those Buckhorns," she said contemptuously. "Not one of those young'uns has a warm coat to her name, and here they are all decked out in white fur mittens that won't last till dinner time. And white boots!" She wrinkled her nose.

"But they're so pretty, Ma. Can't I take Burpy Betty out to show 'em, Ma?" Caroline asked.

"Well, all right. But mind you take care of her."

Caroline buttoned up her brown coat—made over from the one Ethan wore last winter. She zipped up her brown boots, bought two sizes too big so they'd last an extra year, and hurried out with Burpy Betty wrapped in her pink blanket.

Half an hour later she was back, crying and screaming, "I'm never going to play with them again."

Burpy Betty's blanket was wet and dirty, and one sleeve of her frilly dress hung from her shoulder by a single thread. Her pretty cap was gone, and her yellow hair was wet and stuck out in stiff little points all over her head.

"Whatever in the world happened?" Ma asked.

It took a while to find out that the Buckhorns had grabbed Burpy Betty away from Caroline and fought over her. By the time Caroline got her back, she didn't look like a new doll any more and Caroline cried most of the rest of the afternoon.

The whole week after Christmas it rained—when it didn't snow—and they were all inside under each other's feet all the time. Before vacation was over, Jeremy was almost wishing for school to start. He got tired of fooling with the Zoomer, but Ethan and Johnson never did.

Homer D. never did take to building anything with his blocks, but he liked to take them out of the box and scatter them around. What with the blocks on the floor and the slot cars racing back and forth, it was almost as hard to get across the floor as it was to cross the street, and pretty near as dangerous.

Caroline's doll buggy stood in a corner with one wheel off—ever since the day Ma didn't notice her dragging it down the steps. The wheel came off before she got the buggy all the way down, and Pansy Buckhorn grabbed it and started rolling it down the alley. She came back hollering that a big boy snatched the wheel away from her, and Caroline never did get it back. That was another bad afternoon. They like to never got Caroline to stop crying.

About the only thing that looked the same as it had on Christmas morning was the mountain picture hanging over the TV set. Every time Jeremy looked at it, his feet got to itching to walk in some pine needles.

Caroline's bank got broken two days after Christmas. She never had any money anyhow; as soon as she got a nickel, she spent it for candy or bubble gum. But Ethan and Johnson sometimes saved theirs for a day or two, and once in a while Jeremy thought they might put some in the banks. Every night before he went to bed, he shook their banks, but there was never any sound of metal clinking against pottery.

One night after he'd shaken the empty banks, he said crossly to Johnson, "We'll never get back home if it depends on you."

Johnson looked at him sleepily out of one eye. "Why're you always moonin' about Stony Crick? What's wrong with here?"

Jeremy felt sick. He guessed he'd really known that's how they felt, but as long as nobody came right out and said it, he could some way not believe it. How about Pa and Ma? Had they changed, too?

It was hard enough to sleep most nights without having that to worry about. Every time he almost dropped off, the tail of Homer D.'s dumb horse switched across his face or the buckle on its saddle poked him in the ribs. Homer D. still wouldn't sit on that horse, but he carried it everywhere, even to bed.

In the morning, Caroline was fussing over Burpy Betty's doll carriage. It wasn't going to be easy to find out how Caroline felt about going home.

Finally he asked, "Do you think Burpy Betty'll like it in Stony Crick?"

"Oh, she wouldn't like to leave home," Caroline said.

"She wouldn't like it without a bathroom. She has to have a bath every day."

That was the worst thing yet. Caroline had called Chicago "home."

Ma was cooking breakfast, and Jeremy peeked into the cupboard where she kept the jar full of Stony Crick money. It was about half-full of quarters and dimes and even a few dollar bills.

"Ma," Jeremy asked, "do you think there's a chance we might get back by summer?"

Ma gave him a quick look. "I shouldn't wonder," she said. So that much was all right. Surely Ma and Pa would think alike about anything as important as going back home.

One night right after New Year's, Pa came in the door looking white and cross.

"Turn that thing off," he snapped at Johnson. Usually he sat down to watch TV while Ma lifted up supper.

Johnson hurried over to turn off the TV set, and Pa dropped down on the sofa and looked at nothing the way Homer D. did sometimes.

Ma hurried over to him. "Why, Will, what's the matter?" she asked. "Are you sick?"

"I sure am," Pa said. "Sick as I'll ever be. I'm out of work again."

"Out of work?" Ma asked, her freckles showing up against her white skin. "How could you be? Mr. Keller said you'd have a job as long as ever he was there."

"That's just it. He's not goin' to be there. He's sold out; they're goin' to build a big apartment buildin' on that corner. One more week and the station's closed for good. But it ain't the end of everythin'. I found jobs before and I'll find 'em again."

"Will," Ma said, "why don't we just take what we got and go home. We'll manage some way."

Jeremy held his breath.

"What with?" Pa asked. "Besides, I ain't so sure we'd ought to go back to Stony Crick. And even if we was to, we couldn't do it whilst we owe money here."

Ma looked at the TV set and the big sofa like she hated them. "We got no business owin' money," she said. "It's what happens every time folks rustle around in unpaid-for silk."

"I just wanted you to have the things we never had before," Pa told her.

"There's more to livin' than things," Ma said, "and you was always the first to say so back home."

There was more talk, but Jeremy didn't hear it. Now he knew. Pa'd come right out and said maybe they wouldn't be going back to Stony Crick. Ever.

# 13

## Some Better—Some Worse

"Hurry up!" Jeremy called over his shoulder.

It was the first day of school after Christmas vacation, and Ethan and Johnson kept lagging behind. But of course they didn't have the call to go fast that he did; they weren't in Mrs. McNutt's room. If there was anything she hated more than Kentucky, it was being late. It didn't seem fair to have to stay a whole hour after school for being two minutes late, and sitting alone in a room with Mrs. McNutt for an hour was like a whole day with anybody else.

The snow was coming down like it was being poured out of a giant milk pan, and no matter which way he turned his head the wind made his nose and ears ache. He hadn't had time to put on his boots, and his feet felt as stiff as two frozen fish. Now he could see that the traffic guards were still at the corner; maybe he'd make it.

He was half a block ahead of Ethan and Johnson, almost at the school corner, when his feet slid out from under him, and he landed flat on his back. His books were scattered in a circle around him, and when he sat up he could see his arithmetic homework paper crumpled up under a snow-weighted shrub. He'd copied that stupid paper twice so Mrs. McNutt couldn't fault him for having a messy one. She hated messy papers even more than she hated Kentucky and being late. By the time he got up, everyone had gone in. If the rest of the day turned out as bad as the beginning, he might as well turn around and go home right now.

No use to hurry. He might as well be hung for a sheep as a lamb. His steps got slower and slower the closer he got to his room. Of course the door was shut now, solid and forbidding in front of him just the way it had been the first day he came. He had to stretch out his hand twice before he could turn the knob. Once inside, he braced himself to hear Mrs. McNutt's icy voice ask if the Weatherheads didn't own a clock. When nothing happened, he looked up. Standing at Mrs. McNutt's desk was a teacher with pale yellow hair and a dress to match. She didn't look to be much taller than he was and she was smiling at him.

"You must have had a hard time getting here this morning," she said. "You'd better put your shoes with the other wet ones by the radiator." Sure enough, there was a long row of wet shoes under the window. What would Mrs. McNutt say when she got back? The last thing she would want was to have anybody take their shoes off in her room.

He noticed Nick and Joe had theirs off, too, so there wouldn't be anyone making fun of him.

As soon as he sat down, the lady said, "My name is Miss Lynn, and I will be your teacher the rest of the year."

Darlene waved her hand in the air. "Where's Mrs. McNutt?"

"Mrs. McNutt moved to California with her husband. He's been very sick. I know it's hard to lose your teacher in the middle of the year, but we'll have to do the best we can."

Jeremy tried to feel sorry about losing Mrs. McNutt, but he couldn't. He was sorry about her husband, though. Maybe that's what made Mrs. McNutt so cross.

As usual, he'd missed the beginning of what the teacher was saying. ". . . and so I thought each one of you could tell me about yourself; then I'd know something besides just your names." She looked at the roll book. "Nick Adroski."

For some reason Nick didn't swagger the way he usually did.

"What do you want me to say?" he asked.

"Anything you like. Tell us about your family and what you like to do."

Jeremy couldn't figure out why Nick was standing all hunched over. Then he could see there was a big hole in one of Nick's brown socks. Two bare toes stuck out and he was trying to cover them with his other foot. No wonder he couldn't think of anything to say.

Miss Lynn tried to prime the pump. "What do you like to do?"

Jeremy wondered what Nick could find to say he liked to do that wasn't ornery. Finally he blurted out, "I like to sing." He glared at the class as if daring them to laugh, but Miss Lynn looked so interested that he went on, "Mom buys records, and sometimes we sing together."

Jeremy always thought Nick was as tough as a boiled owl. He couldn't imagine him even having a mother, let alone singing with her.

After that Jeremy. listened closely. He found out all kinds of things he didn't know about the class. Darlene had eight brothers and sisters younger than she was. No wonder she always tried to rule the roost. A lot of people didn't have fathers that lived with them, and some didn't have a mother or father either one. Ben lived with his aunt and five cousins, and Alvin lived with his grandmother. Jeremy tried to imagine what it would be like without Pa or Ma. He kept thinking about Nick singing with his mother. What made him so mean once he got away from home?

When Miss Lynn called, "Jeremy Weatherhead," he almost didn't mind walking up to the front. He didn't know exactly what there was about Miss Lynn that made him want her to know about Stony Crick and the mountains and Ma and Pa and Mr. Sherman.

Miss Lynn never faulted him once on the way he talked. In fact, when he said Caroline was so little she had to stand twice to make a shadow, the teacher smiled and said, "What an interesting way to say it." That made him feel so good he went on to tell her about some of the things he missed from home, like water from the tin dipper at the spring where the moss grew so thick and carpety instead of what came out of the faucet here in Chicago. The best part was that for once he got to finish what he started.

While he was on vacation, Jeremy wouldn't have believed he'd ever be in a hurry to get to school, but now he hurried off every morning without even waiting for Ethan and Johnson. Even the room was different with Mrs. McNutt gone. Instead of writing things on the board like, "An untidy desk means an untidy mind," Miss Lynn wrote poems, and she put up a new picture almost every day. Miss Lynn's pictures were just to look at. The class didn't have to memorize who painted them and why, the way they did when Mrs. McNutt put one up.

By the end of January things were about as good as they could be in Chicago. Mr. Keller had sold out the garage right after New Year's, but Fenn had finally got Pa a job in the place where he worked. It was the most money Pa had ever made, but he purely hated that job.

Pa knew how to take a whole car apart and put it back together again so it was better than ever, but all day long now his job was to screw two little pieces of metal together. And Fenn had warned him that he'd better be on time every blessed day because there were three men looking for every job there was.

"Don't seem worth gettin' up in the morning for," Pa said. "You never see what you make, and every day it's the same as the day before." But Pa wasn't one to complain. He only said it once, and if he was tireder at night than when he really worked hard and if he didn't talk much any more, at least he and Ma didn't need to fault each other about money.

At school nobody'd called Jeremy "Leatherhead" for some time. Once in a while somebody even acted like they'd be his partner for lunch, but he always turned his head away and walked by himself at the end of the line. If there was one thing he'd learned in Chicago, it was never to trust anybody his own age, so nobody was going to find out that he cared about walking alone.

A few weeks after Miss Lynn came, Ma asked Jeremy if he'd like to invite her home for supper—the way they'd done with teachers back home.

This was such a daring idea that he had to think it over for several days before he decided. Then it took several more days for him to get up the courage to ask her.

"She can't do more than say no," Ma reminded him sensibly.

Miss Lynn didn't say no, but right away he wished she

had. How would Ethan and Johnson act? What would she think about Homer D.? What would they talk about at the table?

Ma was happier than she'd been for a long time. She washed the curtains and she must have planned six different meals.

"Do you think Miss Lynn would like fried chicken or boiled chicken best?" she would ask.

Jeremy wasn't much help. "She'll like whatever you cook," he told her.

Ma decided that since they were having a company dinner, they might as well invite Mr. Sherman. Jeremy was glad enough to have him, but he wished he'd leave Baron at home. Nobody else knew how he felt about Baron, but Miss Lynn had a way of understanding things.

Sometimes he looked forward to the Friday night she was coming, and sometimes he dreaded it. But, however he felt about it, the day finally got there.

He hurried home from school. Miss Lynn wouldn't be coming until six o'clock. When he ran up the stairs and opened the door, the rich golden smell of chicken and dumplings was filling the air. The battered yellow table was in the center of the room, covered with Ma's hand-loomed white tablecloth Grandma Fickle had left for her. The tablecloth was too long for the little table and hung down on the floor, but it looked rich and elegant. An angel food cake that must have been a mile high stood proudly in the center of the table, and Grandma's blue moon-and-stars compote stood beside it, filled with shimmery red jelly. They hadn't had an angel food cake since they'd left home. Ma'd really been putting the big pot in the little one for Miss Lynn.

Ma was stirring something on the stove, and her cheeks were pink. She had on her navy-blue church dress. Jeremy hadn't seen her wear that since they'd left home.

Every Sunday Ma'd said, "We'd ought to find us a church," but somehow they never did. Pa'd worked most Sundays when he was at the filling station, and Ma'd never gone to church without Pa. Some ways Ma was timid. But every Sunday morning she lined them all up and read a chapter of the gospel to them. And she wouldn't let them go outside until noon. "If we can't go to church, at least you're not going to run up and down the street like heathens," she told them.

Caroline wasn't any problem. She loved to dress up for company. As soon as she got home, she put on her pink dress with the ruffles around the bottom, and tied pink ribbons on her pigtails, and sat on the sofa so she wouldn't muss anything up.

"Who do you think you are? Company?" Ma asked. But she was smiling.

Ethan and Johnson were something else. Jeremy had to shine their shoes for them and make them wash their hands over again. He stood over them until they'd slicked their hair down with water. He spruced Homer D. up at the same time.

"What's so great about Miss Lynn?" they wanted to know. "Don't you get enough of her six hours a day?"

Pa was late getting home, and when he saw the company table, he groaned. "I'm too tired to make company talk," he said, but he went into the bedroom and came back wearing his good shirt and tie.

Right at six o'clock there was a knock at the door, and Mr. Sherman and Miss Lynn stood there together.

"Where's Baron?" Ethan asked.

"I don't take him to a party unless I have to," Mr. Sherman explained.

At least everything was starting right, Jeremy thought.

Miss Lynn looked beautiful in a red coat and a dress the same color. Jeremy took her coat into the bedroom, and Caroline followed him. She patted the coat. "Isn't it pretty? And her little golden earrings and her golden bracelet and her shoes with the little bows?" Jeremy didn't see how Caroline had memorized it all so fast.

Ma had a real family-reunion dinner, and it turned out that everything they had was just what Miss Lynn liked best. Even the black-eyed peas. And she said Ma made the best dumplings she ever ate, and the best angel food cake, too.

After dinner Pa had to go back to work. Miss Lynn was bound to help Ma wash the dishes, and the two of them didn't seem to have any trouble finding something to talk about.

After the dishes were put away, Ma went into the bedroom, and Miss Lynn sat down on the sofa with her eyes sparkling. "I've persuaded Mrs. Weatherhead to show me some of the quilts she's made," she said to Mr. Sherman. "My grandmother made any number of them. She left one to me, and I'd like to use it, but I'm so afraid something will happen to it that I keep it in a box under my bed."

Ma came back, her arms full. "There's no wear-out to a good quilt," she said.

"Oh, how beautiful!" Miss Lynn gasped. Ma'd put her piney quilt on top. It was Jeremy's favorite, because on each block was pieced a tiny green pine tree.

"It looks like a miniature forest," Miss Lynn was saying to Mr. Sherman. He ran his long fingers appreciatively over a block. Jeremy was proud of Miss Lynn for not just letting him sit there like a bump on a log, not knowing what they were talking about.

"And this next one's called 'Bear's Paw'. " Ma pulled a red-and-white quilt off the stack.

"For goodness' sake," Miss Lynn said, "that's just like the one my grandmother gave me, only mine's yellow and white, and she called it 'Hand of Friendship.' "

Jeremy looked at it critically. "Looks more like a bear's paw than a hand of friendship to me."

Mr. Sherman had quickly run his fingers over this pattern, too. "Unless the friendly hand only had four fingers," he said.

"Some folks call it 'Duck's-Foot-in-the-Mud,' " Ma told them.

Ethan and Johnson had gone outside at the first glimpse of the quilts, but Caroline sat on the floor by Miss Lynn and hardly took her eyes off her. Even Homer D. sat by her instead of going off in a corner with his blocks, the way he usually did.

"That next one's just the 'Shoo Fly,' " Ma said. "I cut my sewing teeth on that one. The pattern's not much—just nine patches of about anything to the block, but how we all saved up our scraps to trade."

Jeremy was amazed at Ma. He'd never heard her talk so much before. He was proud, too. He'd always thought Ma's quilts were pretty enough, but he'd supposed they were something that everybody had.

Suddenly Miss Lynn looked at Ma. "I have a wonderful idea," she said. "But I'm not going to tell you about it until I find out for sure."

One day during the next week Miss Lynn told Jeremy

she had something she wanted to tell Ma. "If you'll wait a few minutes," she told him, "I'll drive you home."

Jeremy had seen funny little cars like Miss Lynn's, but he'd never expected to ride in one. He hoped Ethan and Johnson would be out front when they got home, but there wasn't a soul around but Pansy Buckhorn, who stuck her tongue out at them and disappeared around the corner of the house.

He could tell Ma was really glad to see Miss Lynn. She didn't say she wanted to talk to Ma alone, so he stayed quietly nearby. She started talking almost before she sat down. "I had to be sure I was right before I said anything to you. But would you be interested in making quilts to sell?"

"I never thought about it." Ma sounded pleased. "Who'd buy them?"

"I have a friend, Jane Conrad, who's a social worker in this neighborhood." Ma stiffened at the words "social worker," but Miss Lynn went right on. "She realized that there must be dozens of people in this area who know how to make these exquisite quilts, and there are hundreds of other people who would like to own them. One of the churches in the neighborhood has agreed to let Jane use a room to set up quilt frames. Would you be interested in helping? The profit would be divided among the workers."

"You mean go to an old-fashioned quiltin' bee and get paid for it?" Ma's eyes lighted up.

"I suppose it would be something like that."

That was the beginning of the change in Ma.

Two or three days a week she went to the big, red-brick Methodist church down the street. She came home full of talk about running vines and feather stitches and Ella Bargel and Wanda Martin.

Sometimes she and Homer D. weren't even there when Jeremy got home from school, but on those days she was sorry and always cooked something special for dinner. She laughed more, and she didn't grab their clothes to stick them in the washtub the way she did at first when she was so heartsick for Stony Crick, but at least once in a while he could wear a shirt long enough for it to get comfortable.

Now even Ma had friends, the same as Ethan and Johnson and Caroline, and he was the only one left out in the cold, without a friend his own age. He was never going to amount to anything here in this place, and maybe they'd never be anyplace else. Maybe he'd be "Leather-head" all his life, doing everything wrong, laughed at, and walking alone. He might as well make up his mind to it.

# 14

## Hook, Line, and Sinker

"Five dollars. Five dollars and ten cents." Jeremy shook the jar hard, but only one more penny came out. "Five dollars and eleven cents," he said.

"Is that right?" Ma asked, but she wasn't really listening. She hardly ever counted the money in the Stony Crick jar any more unless he asked her to. She was too busy with her quilting bees and was still always talking about Ella Bargel and Wanda Martin and what they said.

Once there'd been almost twenty dollars in the jar, but then Pa'd been laid off for two weeks by a strike, and Ma'd had to use the money for the payments on the TV and sofa and the icebox. She still said she wanted to go back to Stony Crick, but sometimes Jeremy wondered if she really did. Pa'd never said for sure they wouldn't go back, and as long as nobody ever put such a thing into words, Jeremy could go on acting like nothing was changed. There was no need to worry about Ethan and Johnson and Caroline spoiling things by talking about it. They never seemed to so much as give Stony Crick a thought.

He didn't even think the rest of them knew Ma had any Stony Crick money till one Saturday morning when the boys were on their way to the grocery for Ma. When they turned the corner, Jeremy saw Nick leaning against the brick wall of the drugstore. He was busy counting a wad of paper money he'd taken out of a shabby billfold.

"Wow!" Ethan said. "I never saw so much money."

Nick looked up from his counting. "Oh, that's not so much," he said. "There's a lot more where that came from. My old lady has stacks more stashed away under her mattress. I'll bet your old lady does, too."

"No, she don't," Ethan said.

Johnson spoke up. "She keeps hers in a glass jar."

"She's got a lot of it, though," Ethan had to put in.

"C'mon, Ma was in a hurry for that flour." Jeremy pushed them along the street. It wasn't anybody's business what Ma did with her money.

The weather stayed nice all that week. The snow had melted and the sun was warm for March. Ethan and Johnson never came straight home from school the way Jeremy did, and these days they stayed out till supper time every night. That week they didn't have much to say when they did get home, and they didn't eat the way they usually did. They didn't even fight.

Ma got to looking at them sort of worried. "I sure wish I knew where to get some sassafras," she said. "I'd brew up some tea and pour it down those two. I never knew 'em to look so peaked and to pick at their food thataway. They sure need a good spring tonic."

"I'm glad you don't know where to get it," Johnson said. "Most springs we have to drink it till we slosh."

"Slosh," Homer D. said happily, "slosh, slosh."

Friday afternoon when Jeremy got home from school, Ma was sitting on the sofa watching the door. The look on her face almost made him turn tail and back out, but he couldn't think of anything he'd done.

"What's wrong, Ma?" he asked. "Is something wrong?"

"It's the money," she said. "All but one of the bills is gone out of the glass jar."

"Maybe Pa took 'em," Jeremy said.

"No, he don't know what happened to them, either. For the life of me I don't see how anybody could've got in or how they'd know where to look if they did."

Jeremy thought about Nick leaning up against the drugstore wall, counting his money. What was it Johnson had said to him? "She keeps hers in a glass jar," he'd told Nick. But Jeremy didn't say anything to Ma about it. He'd have to think it over.

Jeremy didn't know when he'd seen Ma sit quiet for so long, but after a while she got up and started to fix supper, moving slow, not singing and rattling pans like she usually did.

Ethan and Johnson didn't come in till after Pa did.

"Did you find the money?" Pa asked Ma right off.

"What money?" Caroline asked, but she went over and started fussing over Burpy Betty without waiting for an answer.

"How could I find it?" Ma asked. "It's gone, and that's all there is to it."

At the supper table it seemed like they couldn't talk about anything but the money. Jeremy didn't want to get Ethan in trouble, but finally he just had to tell what happened on Saturday. He hated to have Ethan and Johnson look at him while he was telling it, but they didn't anyhow. They just kept staring down at their plates like they'd never seen them before.

"Oh, it don't seem likely that boy could've got in," Ma

said. "Besides, if he did, why wouldn't he take the whole jar instead of just those six bills? And he didn't even know where you live, did he?"

"It was only five, Ma," Johnson said. Ethan glared at him, and Johnson put his hand over his mouth.

"Johnson Weatherhead," Pa thundered, "you begin right now and tell me everythin' you know about that money."

"We was just tryin' to get more for you and Ma," Ethan said. "We didn't steal it. You know we wouldn't steal it."

"We didn't know it would turn out the way it did," Johnson put in. "He promised us twenty or thirty dollars."

"But there was only newspaper in that envelope."

"He said his uncle wanted it."

"All right, let's start at the other end. I want the truth and I want every bit of it now." Pa's voice meant business.

"You'd better tell the truth," Caroline said, "or blisters'll come out on your tongue."

"Tongue." Homer D. chuckled, sticking his tongue out as far as it would go.

"Hush," Ma said. "Give the boys a chance to talk."

It took the boys quite a while to get their story out.

Monday they'd been on their way home from school when they saw a billfold on the sidewalk in front of them.

Just as Johnson picked it up, an older boy they'd never seen before ran across the street toward them. "Hey, I saw that first," he said.

"Is it yours?" Ethan asked him.

"No," he said. "I was just goin' to pick it up. Let's see what's in it."

There wasn't anything in it but a dirty little piece of pink paper with a number written on it in pencil.

"Oh, it's a pawn ticket," the boy said.

"What's that?" Ethan asked.

The boy told them that when a person needed money he could take anything he had that was worth something to a pawn shop. Say you had a gold watch. The man in the shop would give you some money and keep your watch. He'd give you a ticket, and when you wanted your watch back again, all you had to do was to give back the money you'd borrowed and hand him the ticket. But if you left anything there too long, he'd sell it.

"What do you suppose they traded for this ticket?" Johnson asked.

"Let's go see," the boy said. "Sometimes they put things in the window if they've had them a long time."

They walked several blocks and finally stopped in front of a dirty window with "Pawn Shop" written on it in gold. In the window was a hodgepodge of cameras and suitcases and trumpets and drums and other things.

"Look over there," the boy said excitedly. "There's what's on the ticket! The number matches. It's an electric guitar."

"I don't see any number," Johnson said.

"Well, it's there, whether you see it or not."

"We don't need a guitar even if we had any money, and we don't. Let's go home."

"Hey, I've got an idea! My uncle's been looking for a guitar, and he'd pay as much as fifty or sixty dollars for a good one. I'll bet we could get this one out of hock for a lot less than that. We could sell it to my uncle and make a lot of money."

"We told you we didn't have any money."

"I don't either, but I could get some and get it over here before anybody misses it. You must know where you could get some. Old folks are always stashing money away somewhere."

The boys looked at each other. Ma's jar!

"You look like you've thought of something. I figured you would. Get back here with all the money you can, and I'll get mine. I'll meet you at the drugstore."

"We can't get it if Ma's home," Johnson told him.

"Well, if she is, I'll meet you at the drugstore the same time tomorrow."

Nobody was home, but even so the boys could hardly take the money out of the jar. It seemed like stealing even if it wasn't, but they kept thinking how Ma's face would look when she found twenty or thirty dollars in her jar instead of five. Maybe they wouldn't even tell her for a while where it came from—just let her guess.

They hurried back to the drugstore with the five one-dollar bills wadded up into a tight little ball, and the boy was waiting there for them.

"How much didja get?" he asked.

"Five dollars," Johnson said proudly.

"It's not much, but maybe it'll do." He held out his hand.

Johnson hesitated. "We don't even know your name," he said. "I don't know if we should give you Ma's money."

The boy laughed. "Good thinkin'," he said. "My name's Roy Sears, but you're right not to give money to a stranger. I figured you were too smart for that, so here's what I'll do. I'll put ten dollars in this envelope. You take it home, and I'll meet you here tomorrow with the money I get from the guitar. You know I'll show up because I already gave you five dollars more than you gave me." He took a ten-dollar bill out of his pocket, carefully sealed it up in an envelope, and gave it to Johnson. Johnson slowly handed him the five dollars and the pawn ticket.

"See you tomorrow," Roy called, hurrying off down the street.

On Tuesday Ethan and Johnson could hardly wait till school was out. They waited on the corner for Roy till dark. He never came, and when they opened the envelope he'd handed them there wasn't anything in it but some cut-up pieces of newspaper. They'd walked back past the pawn shop and the guitar was still in the window. How Roy had switched envelopes, they didn't know.

Nobody said a word all the time Ethan and Johnson were talking. Finally Pa said, "Looks like you boys swallowed a story—hook, line, and sinker. You ain't the first nor yet the last, but there's two things that bothers me. In the first place, you kept that ticket—somethin' that didn't belong to you, even if it wasn't worth anythin'— and in the second place, you took Ma's money without askin'."

"The whole thing wouldn't ever have happened if we'd stayed in Stony Crick where such folks don't lay in wait in the streets," Ma said. "Anyhow, the boys don't have enough to keep them busy here, and idleness and sin are twins."

"Maybe we shouldn't never have come," Pa said, "but we're here, and there's no way to get back now. We got to do the best we can where we are."

# 15

## "Sit and Stay"

"The blue one's mine."

"That was yesterday. Today it's mine."

"You said I could have a car today." Caroline stood in the middle of the track with her hands on her hips.

"That was yesterday, too. That one's broke now."

Caroline snatched the blue car out of Ethan's hand and ran across the floor with it. Ethan and Johnson thudded after her, yelling. Caroline got the bedroom door open and slammed it shut just in time.

"Ma!" she hollered. "They won't let me play."

They could hear the familiar thumping of Mrs. Quill's broom on the ceiling of her apartment. That always got Ma's dander up, but Jeremy had to admit Mrs. Quill had plenty to thump about these days. For two weeks now Pa'd made Ethan and Johnson come straight home from school and play in the yard without any friends. Since that only left a passel of girls for them to play with, they spent most of their time in the house, running the slot cars, and fighting, and playing the TV as loud as it would go, and teasing Caroline. It was some quieter now that the Buckhorns had gone home for one of their visits, but this still wasn't exactly a good place to read in.

Jeremy tucked *Huckleberry Finn* under his arm and was headed for the stairs when Homer D. shambled over and stuck something in his hand. How in the world had Homer D. got hold of a pencil?

"A." Homer D. grinned up at him. "A."

Wouldn't you know Homer D. would pick now for the first time in his life to want to talk about ABC's, when Jeremy couldn't wait to get out of the noise and find out what was going to happen next to Huck Finn?

"I'll be back pretty soon," he promised Homer D., his hand on the doorknob. But the look on Homer D.'s face really had him in between a rock and a hard place.

"All right, Homer D.," he said, putting the book down slowly. "All right, I'll find a piece of paper."

The way it turned out, Homer D. wasn't really all that anxious to work on ABC's. Jeremy guessed what Homer D. really wanted was just some attention from him. Going to Mr. Sherman's apartment had kept Jeremy from feeling quite so left out, but Homer D. had been left out all his life. Jeremy felt shamed.

It didn't take much to satisfy Homer D. After a few minutes, he yawned and went over to get his horse, and Jeremy picked up his book and raced downstairs. He hoped Mr. Sherman would be home.

When he knocked, he could hear Baron's toenails clicking across the floor. Then Mr. Sherman said, "Sit and stay," and opened the door. When Jeremy was curled up in one of the big chairs, it seemed as if he was a world away from the noisy apartment upstairs. Even Baron didn't bother him much any more. He still raised his head every time Jeremy made a sudden move, but now he knew the big dog wasn't going to spring at him.

One of the things that made him comfortable with Mr. Sherman was that he was ready to listen if Jeremy wanted to talk, but he never asked questions. This was one of the days when they didn't talk much. Jeremy read while Mr. Sherman typed some letters.

"There's a bowl of peanuts on the telephone table by your chair. Help yourself," Mr. Sherman told him.

Then everything was quiet except for the tapping of the typewriter. Every few minutes Jeremy reached out for a handful of nuts without taking his eyes from his book.

" . . . Then away out in the woods I heard that kind of a sound that a ghost makes when it wants to tell about something that's on its mind and can't make itself understood, and can't rest easy in its . . ."

There was a crash and a ringing noise, and Baron jumped up with a yelp. Jeremy jumped out of his chair and stepped on Baron's foot. The big dog growled at him with his teeth showing, the way he had the first day he'd seen him. Jeremy felt cold, but there was sweat on his forehead and his tongue felt too big for his mouth. He backed around so the big chair was between him and Baron. It was a good thing Mr. Sherman heard the noise because Jeremy couldn't say a word.

"Baron, sit and stay," Mr. Sherman said. "What happened, Jeremy?"

Jeremy could speak now that he was standing behind the chair with Baron on the other side of it. "I guess I must've knocked the telephone off the table and it fell on Baron, and then I stepped on his foot."

"Then he's growling because his foot hurts. Also, he doesn't like surprises. He's not growling at you."

But Jeremy wasn't so sure. Now he was right back where he started as far as Baron was concerned. He jumped every time Baron moved all the rest of the afternoon. And every time he jumped, Baron raised his head and looked at him warningly.

That night he lay awake after the others had gone to sleep. It was kind of nice being the only one awake, with the house so quiet. He always used to think about Stony Crick whenever he had time. He remembered how Ma said it didn't pay to look back, and he tried not to, but it didn't always work. It seemed like Stony Crick was hazier in his mind all the time, though. When he thought about school now, he didn't see the weather-beaten, gray building at home any more; he saw the ugly, red-brick school he went to now.

Baron was barking, and Jeremy realized slowly that he had been for quite a while. This was the first time he'd ever heard him bark in the night; Mr. Sherman never let him bark more than once or twice even in the daytime. Something had to be wrong.

Jeremy climbed out of bed, trying not to wake up Homer D. He didn't have to worry about Ethan and Johnson; they wouldn't wake up even if he stepped on them. He almost had to holler when he stepped on one of Homer D.'s blocks while he was tiptoeing through the living room, but he didn't. He opened the inside door and slipped out into the hall. There wasn't anything to be seen and nothing to be heard except Baron's barking, but Jeremy still couldn't get over the feeling that something was

*132*

wrong. He was just closing the door again when he realized what it was. Smoke! Or was it just in his mind, the way it had been so many times since their house had burned? He sniffed again. No, it really was smoke.

He ran through the living room and into the bedroom. "Pa! Ma! Wake up! I smell smoke."

Pa just laid there like a log, but Ma raised up on one elbow. "What's wrong, Jeremy?"

"It's smoke, Ma. It is! Come out in the hall and you can smell it."

Ma sighed. She got out of bed and padded toward the hall, but he could tell by the way she walked that she didn't think anything was really wrong. When she opened the door, though, the smell was stronger than it had been before.

The hall seemed the same as always, but when he looked over the bannister he could see little wisps of smoke curling up from downstairs.

"Will! Will!" Ma was running toward the bedroom now. "Get up! There's a fire downstairs."

Pa stood in the bedroom doorway in his long underwear. Caroline was holding onto one of his legs and hollering.

By this time they could hear Mrs. Quill out in the yard screaming, "Get out! Get out! The house is on fire!"

"Grab what you can and git!" Pa said. He had his hands full trying to get Homer D. to let go of his horse. Finally he just picked him up and started down the stairs with the horse wrapped around both their necks. He grabbed Caroline's hand. She already had Burpy Betty in her arms; she slept with her.

Ethan and Johnson unplugged the TV set and were trying to push it toward the door.

"Leave that be," Ma hollered at them. She was carrying two coats and the money jar. Now smoke was coming under the door in little wisps.

Jeremy grabbed the mountain picture off the wall and followed Ma down the steps. The yard was full of people. A few, wearing coats and sweaters over their nightclothes, had run over from the apartment house next door.

Mrs. Quill was screaming, "Mr. Sherman's in his room. I couldn't get any answer out of him, and he hasn't come out."

"I'll git him," Pa said. He set Homer D. and the horse down and ran up the front steps and into the hall. He banged on Mr. Sherman's door, but there was no answer except for Baron, who'd never stopped barking for a minute.

Pa rattled the doorknob. "You got the key?" he called out to Mrs. Quill, who was standing at the bottom of the steps with Jeremy and Jean Elizabeth right behind her.

"Here in my purse," she said, fumbling in the black leather bag that always hung from her arm.

"I know where it is," Jean Elizabeth piped up surprisingly. She yanked at the purse. Her mother grabbed for it, and one leather strap broke. A jumble of keys and letters and coins poured out at Mrs. Quill's feet, and Jeremy and Jean Elizabeth and Mrs. Quill squatted down and pawed frantically through them in the dark.

"Here it is!" Jean Elizabeth ran up the steps and handed a key to Pa, but that one wouldn't fit. He had to try three more before the door swung open.

They still couldn't see any fire coming from the house, but the smoke was making Pa cough. It seemed to be coming from the stairway. Jeremy couldn't really see what was happening in the house. He ran around Mrs. Quill and up the steps into the hall. He could hear Ma calling for him to come back, but Pa, standing there in the open door of Mr. Sherman's apartment, didn't even notice him. He was looking at Mr. Sherman, stretched out on the floor face down. Baron was standing over him. When he saw Jeremy and Pa standing in the doorway, he growled fiercely. Pa stepped slowly into the room, and Baron bared his teeth.

"You've been down here often enough," Pa said. "Can't you get him to back off?"

Jeremy swallowed. "I'll try," he said. "We got to get Mr. Sherman out some way."

Pa coughed. "Seems like it's only smoke, but a person can die of smoke same as bein' burned." He took another step toward Baron. Baron's lips drew back in a warning snarl. His red gums showed, and the hair stood up on the back of his neck. He was crouched, ready to spring.

"He won't budge," Pa said, wiping his forehead with a handkerchief. "I don't know how long Mr. Sherman can last in there."

The smoke was billowing into the hall now, and Jeremy could hardly keep his eyes open. They couldn't let Mr. Sherman die.

Jeremy took another step into the room. "Here, Baron," he called, trying not to let his voice shake. "Here, boy."

Baron growled again and bent his legs as if he was going to jump at him. Jeremy backed up.

And then he could hear Mr. Sherman's voice as plain as if Mr. Sherman had sat up and said, "You have to make him know you mean what you say."

"Please, God, don't let my voice shake," Jeremy prayed. He knew this would be his last chance.

He took a deep breath and said, "Baron, sit and stay."

*135*

He was surprised to hear his voice sound so much like Mr. Sherman's.

Baron gave him a long, steady look. He went on growling, but he slowly sat down by Mr. Sherman's head and didn't even budge when Pa moved in quietly and picked Mr. Sherman up. They'd got to the door when Jeremy looked back. Baron was still sitting where he'd been ordered to stay.

"Come, Baron," Jeremy called, and the big dog leaped up and followed him. His wet nose touched Jeremy's hand, and without thinking Jeremy scratched his ears. It was the first time he'd ever touched a dog since he'd been bit.

Just as they got Mr. Sherman out on the steps, the fire engine came screaming up, and the firemen ran into the house.

Hours later, after the firemen left and they could go back inside, they found out the fire had been in Mr. Sherman's apartment. But no one could figure out how it had started. The rest of the house was smoked up like a Kentucky ham, but nothing much was hurt. They took Mr. Sherman to the hospital just to be sure he was all right. He and Baron were going to stay with another teacher until his apartment was cleaned up.

The next morning Jeremy wished he had a friend, even Arthur, to tell about the fire and Mr. Sherman and all the excitement, but everything was the same as usual. Nobody paid any attention to him and at school he kept to himself as always.

After recess, Miss Lynn asked, "Jeremy, why didn't you tell us about the fire at your house last night?"

"Nobody asked me about it," Jeremy replied.

"Why don't you tell us about it now? We all know Mr. Sherman and Baron, and we'd like to hear what happened and how firemen put out a fire."

Jeremy felt proud as a dog with two tails. This was something that only he could tell. He stood up and started talking, and the first thing he knew he'd been caught in a trap as easy as a worm under a jay's nest. He'd blabbed all about how he was afraid of Baron and every other dog. Wild horses couldn't have dragged it out of him before, and here he'd laid it out for everybody to laugh at. But now he'd started he might as well finish.

"That was really brave," Darlene said. "Especially if you were scared."

"Who wouldn't be?" Joe asked.

At lunch, Ben and Joe and Nick crowded around him. "How many firemen were there? Did they open a hydrant? Could we see Baron's tricks when he gets home?"

"Baron doesn't do tricks. Mr. Sherman says he's a working dog," Jeremy explained. He thought about saying that he and Mr. Sherman were the only ones Baron would mind, but then he decided that wasn't exactly true since he'd only tried it once.

After school, half the class wanted to walk home with him to see what the house looked like after the fire. He had a notion to tell them to go fry their fish. They hadn't paid him any mind before, and likely they wouldn't again after they forgot about the excitement. Maybe he'd let them tag along this time, but probably tomorrow he'd go back to being "Leatherhead" and making his mistakes by himself.

Maybe that would be the worst mistake of all, though, he thought. It was one he'd been making ever since he came to Chicago. Ma'd always said you had to cut your coat to fit your cloth, and right now his cloth was made in

Chicago, not in Stony Crick. He'd never like it in Chicago if he lived here all his life. He still hoped they'd get back to Stony Crick, and if they didn't, he'd hanker after it as long as he lived, but right now he was here.

Most everybody he'd met up with here had been meaner than dirt, but maybe it was partly his own fault. Every time his feelings had been hurt, he'd pulled in his horns like a snail and kept them pulled in so nobody would know what he was like inside, the way an animal licks a hurt place and won't let anybody come near. If something went wrong, they all likely snapped out at the first thing that came along. He thought about Nick singing with his mother, and about Ben without any mother. Maybe tomorrow they'd be as mean as ever, but at least he'd ought to give them a try.

"You're purely welcome to come along," he said.